"Do you want some coffee?"

Daniel offered, stepping up to the bed.

He sat beside her and instantly Annie was aware of how unnerving his presence was. Her dreams may have been too vague to recall, but the emotions they'd generated made her uncomfortable, restless. It was simply inappropriate for Daniel to be in her bedroom. She could hear her mother chanting number two hundred fifty-three of the *Lady's Litany*: *One never remained alone in one's bedroom with a gentleman other than one's husband.*

But then she wasn't alone. Her two eight-year-old nieces made perfectly adequate chaperones.

"Girls?" Daniel's voice stopped the twins as they pirouetted around the room. "Do your dad a favor and go stack up the cereal dishes, will you?"

As her two chaperones raced through the door, Annie decided that she was being entirely too Victorian. Her flannel nightgown was as conservative as a nun's, and the thick layer of sheets and blankets would surely protect her from Daniel's X-ray vision.

The problem was, who would protect her from her own imagination now that he was within touching range?

Dear Reader:

Happy holidays! Our authors join me in wishing you all the best for a joyful, loving holiday season with your family and friends. And while celebrating the new year—and the new decade!—I hope you'll think of Silhouette Books.

1990 promises to be especially happy here. This year marks our tenth anniversary, and we're planning a celebration! To symbolize the timelessness of love, as well as the modern gift of the tenth anniversary, each month in 1990, we're presenting readers with a *Diamond Jubilee* Silhouette Romance title, penned by one of your all-time favorite Silhouette Romance authors.

In January, under the Silhouette Romance line's *Diamond Jubilee* emblem, look for Diana Palmer's next book in her bestselling LONG, TALL TEXANS series—*Ethan*. He's a hero sure to lasso your heart! And just in time for Valentine's Day, Brittany Young has written *The Ambassador's Daughter*. Spend the most romantic month of the year in France, the setting for this magical classic. Victoria Glenn, Annette Broadrick, Peggy Webb, Dixie Browning, Phyllis Halldorson—to name just a few!—have written *Diamond Jubilee* titles especially for you. And Pepper Adams has penned a trilogy about three very rugged heroes—and their lovely heroines!—set on the plains of Oklahoma. Look for the first book this summer.

The *Diamond Jubilee* celebration is Silhouette Romance's way of saying thanks to you, our readers. We've been together for ten years now, and with the support you've given us, you can look forward to many more years of heartwarming, poignant love stories.

I hope you'll enjoy this book and all of the stories to come. Come home to romance—Silhouette Romance—for always!

Sincerely,

Tara Hughes Gavin
Senior Editor

MARY BLAYNEY

Father Christmas

Published by Silhouette Books New York
America's Publisher of Contemporary Romance

For Tommye, Sara and Judy,
with a nod to the New Jersey Turnpike.
I wouldn't have gotten this far
without you.

SILHOUETTE BOOKS
300 E. 42nd St., New York, N.Y. 10017

ISBN: 0-373-08688-1

First Silhouette Books printing December 1989

Printed in the U.S.A.

Books by Mary Blayney

Silhouette Desire

True Colors #448

Silhouette Romance

Father Christmas #688

MARY BLAYNEY

is originally a child of the East Coast, having lived in New York and Washington, D.C., until her marriage. Then her life changed dramatically. In the last sixteen years her home has ranged from Muskegon, Michigan, to Juneau, Alaska, with visits to New Zealand and Fiji, as well. Mary laughingly says that her list of previous employers is almost as varied as her addresses have been. But now, as a writer, she has found a career as mobile as her family and hopes to use her travels in her future romance novels.

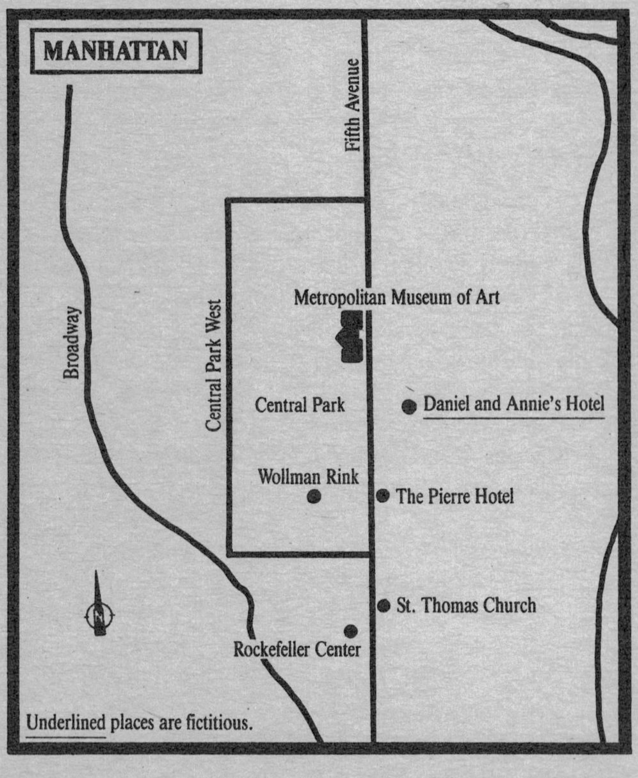
MANHATTAN
Fifth Avenue
Broadway
Central Park West
Metropolitan Museum of Art
Central Park
Daniel and Annie's Hotel
Wollman Rink
The Pierre Hotel
St. Thomas Church
Rockefeller Center
Underlined places are fictitious.

Chapter One

There was no doubt about it. They were two of the most beautiful little girls he'd ever seen. At eight years of age they still had that incredible silver-blond hair they'd been born with and the prettiest blue eyes. They didn't look one bit like him. That hair and those eyes definitely came from their mother.

Daniel Marshall stood in the doorway of his hotel room, all thoughts of his planned outing gone. Kendall and Jessica, his daughters, were less than thirty feet away. He welcomed the same surge of pride and affection he'd felt on the day they were born. It was a relief to know that years of separation hadn't changed his feelings for them.

The girls were busily talking. As anxious as he was to see them, he was reluctant to approach just yet. He wasn't even sure they would recognize him. As much as he hated to admit it, he wanted Annie VerHollan to be there at that first meeting. At this point, Kathy's sister was the only thing he and his daughters had in common.

He observed their flannel nightgowns and outlandish animal slippers—not the usual outfit for a hotel corridor. He could guess what had happened. Stepping out slightly from the shadow of his darkened room, Daniel listened. If he thought they really needed help, he would make his presence known.

"What are we gonna do, Kendall?" There was a tinge of panic in the young voice.

"Gimme a minute to think." Kendall stood with her eyes squeezed shut, concentrating.

Daniel smiled. He could almost feel the child consider and reject options.

"Kendall, how are we gonna get back in?" Jessica hopped impatiently from one foot to the other. Daniel could tell she wasn't excited, just anxious.

"Gimme a minute to think."

"We're locked out. How long is Annie gonna be gone?"

"Just long enough to get stuff for breakfast."

"I want her to come back now."

Daniel tensed in paternal concern at the sound of tears in the young voice. But Kendall seemed to know how to handle the situation and he watched as the older twin patted her sister on the back. It seemed to reassure her and Daniel, too.

"Jessica, honey—" Kendall's voice sounded almost motherly "—please don't worry. I'm sure Annie will think of something if we can't." There was a moment of silence. "I know, she can always get the maid to let us in."

"What maid?" That question was accompanied by a sniffle.

"You know, the one who's gonna make our beds for us. Wow, staying in a hotel is great! I already love it. I wish we could live here forever."

"Not me, Kendall, I already wanna go home. We don't get locked out there. No one locks the door at home."

"I know, Jessie! Let's sing some Christmas songs while we wait. That'll make the time go faster. Should we do 'Jingle Bells' first?"

The tearful twin looked doubtful, but her thin voice joined her sister's hearty one. Daniel smiled at their off-key rendition. They weren't babies anymore, not like they'd been at two years of age when he'd first left for Africa. They weren't even the same kindergartners he'd seen, so briefly, two years ago at their mother's funeral. They still had a lot of growing to do, but Daniel was struck with bitter regret that he'd missed their early years. Kathy was gone now, he reminded himself. But it didn't stop the resentment he felt at the way she'd denied him his children.

Kendall and Jessica were finishing the first chorus, when the elevator doors slid open and Annie VerHollan stepped out. She saw the girls immediately and hurried toward them, not even glancing in his direction. Daniel leaned against the door and took a good look. She could pass for eighteen even though she must be all of twenty-four now.

Annie hadn't changed a bit since he'd last seen her two years ago—the same honey-blond hair, long and straight, now gathered into a ponytail at her nape; the same lithe shape, the pink-and-gray warm-up suit accentuating the curves that were as perfectly proportioned as Daniel remembered them. She really was lovely, in a fresh-faced, open way. She still looked like the cheerleader she'd been in high school. The years had added polish, not really sophistication, but a finish that had turned a pretty girl into a beautiful woman.

Daniel straightened from the doorway, appalled at his thoughts. He'd never noticed Annie like that before, and wondered why it struck him so now. He suppressed the attraction. Instead, he tried to summon the litany of offenses that had fueled their mutual antipathy.

He considered seizing the advantage by calling out to her, then thought better of it. The twins didn't need that. He'd left Annie a note; he would wait for her to call as he'd promised. He slid the door closed quietly, cutting off Kendall's explanation.

"See, we were playing this game, Annie. Jessica and I'd race to see who could push the elevator button first and then run to the room before the door closed. The second time, we didn't make it. Now we're stuck here. We're missing cartoons. You can get the door unlocked, can't you?"

Annie laughed and shook her head in the mildest gesture of rebuke. "Aren't you two lucky that I have my key right here with me? Otherwise we might be stuck out in this hall for a good while, and who wants to eat breakfast standing in the hall of your hotel, hmm?"

She pulled the key out of her pocket. Leaning the bag she was carrying against the wall, Annie wedged the metal into the lock and turned it. As soon as it released, Jessica pushed the door all the way open and held it for her aunt.

With an economy of movement Annie put the few groceries in the refrigerator of the wet bar, pushing the complimentary beer and split of champagne to the back. She served each girl a bowl of cereal, found spoons and put them on the counter, too. The suite came with an amazing assortment of conveniences and she let the children take their cereal over by the TV on the bamboo trays provided so they could watch cartoons while they ate. After all, this was a vacation, wasn't it?

She supposed she should discuss appropriate hotel behavior with them, but right now her mind was too full of other worries. The night manager had confirmed it. Daniel had arrived in the early morning hours. He was right next door and waiting for her call.

She cradled her cup of coffee in both hands and slid onto the stool, observing the girls as they sat laughing at some early-morning madness. They *seemed* unconcerned. Heaven knew they'd spent enough time discussing the fact that their father was arriving today. But maybe it had slipped their minds. They were pretty excited about the holiday, the airplane ride and the New York City adventure.

Kendall and Jessica may have forgotten Daniel's arrival, but she certainly hadn't. Her hands were clammy, her stomach was churning and a vague headache threatened. All that because she had to make a simple phone call. Damnation, how did she get herself into this fix, anyway?

She knew how. All it had taken was one impulsive act. Their lives had been quiet and uneventful until she'd decided to start meddling. But when Daniel had sent that blank check for the girls' Christmas and birthday presents, she'd seen red. The memory could still generate a burst of anger. She loved his two little girls as if they were her own. A blank check—was that really the sum of his feelings for them? Filling in one million dollars had been pure impulse *and* a big mistake.

What had it gotten her? A long-distance phone call from Africa for starters. Despite the static, Daniel's meaning had come through loud and clear. It had also gotten the girls a Christmas with their father. And hadn't that been her goal?

Yes, sir. It had.

This was the chance for father and daughters to get to know each other. True, a meeting on her home ground would have been much more to her liking, but it hadn't been to Daniel's. And as he'd said, he was paying the bills.

With a shrug, Annie tried to dismiss her sense of impending doom and picked up the phone to call him. She could have stepped down the hall and knocked on his door, but today she was chicken enough to put off meeting him face-to-face for as long as possible.

He answered on the first ring. "Marshall."

His voice registered cold and remote.

"Daniel?" Annie cleared her throat and took a deep breath, hoping she sounded mature and in control. "This is Annie VerHollan. I just wanted to let you know that we're here and I'd like to set up a time for all of us to get together."

"Annie, all you have to do is unlock the connecting door. My room opens onto the far end of the suite." The cynically shaded voice reminded her of other conversations—arguments she would just as soon forget.

Instead of shouting *I'm not ready to start living with you*, Annie swallowed the words, cleared her throat once again and tried to sound reasonable. "I guess I could do that, but the girls are watching cartoons right now and I'd like to get them dressed before they see you."

"Annie, if you don't have enough control over them to walk over, turn off the TV and tell them it's time to get dressed..."

"It's not that, Daniel. This is their vacation and I told them they could watch cartoons." Ye gods, she sounded like a simpering idiot, and a defensive one at that.

Apparently Daniel thought so, too. He spoke in a decisive voice, the same tone she imagined he used when he was giving orders in the field. "Annie, I'll be over in an hour. I'm going out to run and then I'll come back for a shower and we'll all go, I don't know, out somewhere."

"Daniel, we have to get some winter coats and then I told the girls we'd go sight-seeing." She hated sounding so tentative. Where was her backbone?

"That would be fine, Annie. Do you think you can have them weaned from the TV by then?"

His sarcastic tone gave Annie all the backbone she needed. Just the cadence of the words reminded her why she hated Daniel Marshall so much. She hung up without comment—and then made a face at the phone for good measure.

She turned to check on the girls, only to find Jessica standing nearby. The child's expression was solemn and a little scared. She looked her aunt in the eye. "Annie, was that our daddy?"

Here was one person who was as nervous as she was. Annie smiled at the sweet face and tried to think positive thoughts about the child's father. "Yes, honey. He'll be here in about an hour."

There was no answering smile and Annie knelt down beside her niece. Her own smile faded. "I guess it's kind of exciting, but a little scary, too, hmm?"

Jessica nodded, her eyes filling with tears. Annie gathered the fragile bundle in her arms and hugged her. Kissing the shining blond head she whispered, "Never forget how much your daddy and I love you. He'll be as proud of you as I am. You wait and see."

Her words seemed to reassure Jessica, who stopped short of crying and took a quivering breath. *Please God,* Annie prayed, *help me make this work.*

With a word to the girls, she slipped into her bedroom to get ready. She couldn't resist the sybaritic pleasure of the sunken tub in the bathroom that she shared with the children. Glad she wasn't the one paying the hot-water bill, she turned on the golden taps to let the cool water warm. She added a handful of the jasmine bath flakes supplied by the hotel and slipped into the water, resting her head on the neck pillow lying on the edge of marble shelf. The hot water loosened her tense muscles and eased the aches generated by the long trip and a restless night's sleep. She took a deep breath and concentrated on relaxing.

An hour was more than enough time for her and the girls to bathe and dress. After all, she didn't have to do dishes or make beds or iron clothes. This holiday had some advantages, after all. She tried to keep the tension away as an image of Daniel intruded. He was definitely not the highlight of this trip. Cripes, why did she always feel so unsettled around him? All of her usual good nature disappeared when she was around Daniel Marshall.

It had been like that from their first meeting a few months before Daniel had married her sister.

Kathy had talked about Daniel constantly from the moment she met him. "He's twenty-one years old, Annie! I mean he's really been around. He was born in New York and grew up in Africa. Now he's in graduate school in Augusta." Annie had to agree he was a real man of the world, or at least as close as they'd ever been to one.

By the time Kathy brought him home to meet their parents, the little town was agog with gossip. He was a looker, Aunt Madge insisted, sexy with real bedroom eyes.

Annie shook her head, sending water rippling around her, as she remembered her fifteen-year-old theatrics. "I don't care if he does strip me with his eyes, I'll just stare him down." Well, it hadn't been anything like that, no sir. As sensitive as she'd been to male reactions, she could tell he had to try hard not to laugh at her when she'd sashayed up to the bar in her very own living room and asked for a glass of wine. He'd handed her a cream soda instead.

It was easy now to identify the negative feeling that had grown around her perception of Daniel Marshall. It was jealousy. She'd been jealous of the man who had so completely captivated her older sister and undermined their close relationship.

Annie had to admit Daniel had done his best to charm her out of her ill-humor. It must have been the perversity of those teen years that had made her refuse those initial overtures. Her friend, Mary Jane, insisted Daniel Marshall was every girl's ideal. He was older and more sophisticated than their high-school boyfriends. Indeed, every time he came to Avon, her friends would find convenient excuses to stop by and say hello. He was always pleasant, with a smile for everyone. In those early days, Annie thought his smile cynical, his friendliness patronizing. Every time one of her friends gushed about him she would shake her head and change the subject.

Annie's animosity had mellowed as the weeks became months. Daniel wasn't her sister's passing fancy. Despite the fact their parents continually discouraged the relationship, Kathy began to talk about a future as Mrs. Daniel Marshall. With the prospect of Daniel as brother-in-law, Annie did her best to overcome her ill feeling. Daniel seemed to welcome the effort. His smile seemed more genuine, his friendliness more sincere.

He went from villain to hero in the space of a day when he and Kathy agreed to take Annie to have her ears pierced even though her parents were opposed to the idea. Parental anger had been an effective bond to the new friendship. Annie smiled, fingering the small pearl studs in her ears, remembering the way Daniel had cheered her small gesture of independence.

When Kathy announced that she was pregnant, and that she and Daniel would marry, Annie thought it the most romantic event in the world. Annie and Kathy's parents predicted no good of the union. Annie ignored their pessimism and helped Kathy plan every detail of the wedding.

It really had been a lovely day, full of happiness and good wishes. Nothing of the ensuing years' pain and separation could dim Annie's memory of the joy she'd shared with Kathy and Daniel.

She had ignored the few snide remarks she'd overheard from some of her older relatives. Obviously those folks had no romance in their souls. As maid of honor, Annie had been thrilled to have a part in such a modern fairy tale. Kathy was in love. Obviously nothing was more important to her sister than being with the man of her dreams, the father of her baby.

Daniel became a hero of impossible proportions.

Annie left for Spain as an exchange student after the baby was born. She wasn't there when the child had died of sudden infant death syndrome. She wanted desperately to come home, but everyone, even Kathy and Daniel, insisted that she stay. Without the day-to-day contact Annie hadn't seen them struggle with their loss. She hadn't seen the way

Kathy's misplaced guilt and Daniel's unexpressed pain had begun to undermine their relationship. Her romantic fantasy remained intact. From her distant vantage point, she reasoned that Daniel and Kathy were a family now; certainly their love would see them through anything.

Another pregnancy had followed two years later, and shortly after the twins' birth, Daniel had left the country while his wife and children stayed behind. The marriage was obviously foundering. Annie listened to Kathy's diatribes and the pendulum of her feelings swung again.

Annie hated him now—hated him for abandoning Kathy, but hated him even more for destroying all her romantic illusions about love and the strength of marriage.

Divorce was inevitable. After a while Kathy pretended Daniel didn't even exist. She would cash the child-support check each month and never mention his name. Daniel seemed to like it that way. He never called or wrote and only came to Avon four years later when news of Kathy's death had reached him by telegram. He'd stayed a mere week, then he'd asked Annie if she would care for his children so he could complete his project. He'd promised it would be only a year, and that he would come home as soon as he could.

Annie had begun to hope he meant to be a real father to his children. She had the girls write letters and send pictures. Daniel had responded in kind. His letters were so different from his conversation, full of anecdotes and silly jokes. She'd begun to look forward to the letters as much as the girls had.

In time, however, she'd noticed that he never mentioned his plans to come home. Her unease grew. One year stretched into two. Her mother had nodded knowingly. It was just what she'd expected of Daniel. Annie defended him, but with less and less conviction. Then one day the blank check had arrived in the mail. It had been an insult, a virtual slap in the face. So Annie had taken matters into her own hands.

Now Daniel was back in their lives. She'd argued with her parents for weeks about this trip, then finally insisted that this was exactly what the girls needed. Even if Daniel never intended to be a father in anything but name, the twins had a right to some of his time, not just his money. She wasn't looking forward to it; she'd admitted that much to her mother. She hadn't expected this to be much of a holiday for her, but it would be special for Kendall and Jessica. For them, she was willing to live with Daniel's arrogance and conceit, at least for the next ten days.

Maybe with the girls as a buffer, Daniel would leave his barbed tongue behind and she could concentrate on making them feel comfortable around their long-absent father. Surely his posting in Africa was almost over. If he didn't accept another contract he could be back in their lives for good. All the tension came flooding back at the thought of losing the girls to his care. *Don't worry about that until you have to.* First she had to get through the next week. And, she reminded herself, it was time to stop reminiscing and start moving.

When the knock came, she was in the girls' bedroom putting the finishing touches on Jessica's hair. Kendall had been standing at the door for the last five minutes and opened it before the echo died. Jessica's worried eyes met Annie's in the mirror. Despite her misgivings, Annie injected all the confidence she could into the smile she gave her niece.

She could hear Kendall chattering in the living room. Annie wasn't worried about how Kendall would react to her father. She would treat him the way she treated every stranger, like a newfound confidant. If he was perceptive at all, it wouldn't take Daniel long to figure out that Kendall babbled when she was nervous or excited, talking about anything and everything. Hurrying through the last of Jessica's toilette, she grabbed the hand of her ever-shy niece and urged her through the door. They walked into the other room in the midst of Kendall's description of the trip from Avon.

"I was sure I was gonna throw up driving to the airport, but Annie invented this really neat adding game and I forgot all about being sick. Then we got to this spot where there was this awful smell and I knew if I wasn't sick then..."

Annie waited for Kendall to wind down and watched Daniel, whose whole attention was focused on his daughter. He was still "a looker," those bedroom eyes still the same shade of blue as the ocean on a sunny day. She supposed the lines around his eyes could have come from smiling the way he was smiling at Kendall now, but Annie liked to think they came from squinting into the sun too much. It was obvious he spent a lot of time outdoors. His skin wasn't really tan, but seemed to be naturally dark, as though years working on an outdoor project had permanently changed his skin tone.

"So Jessica started crying and Annie said she couldn't take her seat belt off, but she could have a pillow, but it was in the overhead compartment. So we had to ask the lady to get it for us. Then Jessie and I had to go to the bathroom, but Annie said she'd wait until..."

Daniel threw Annie a pleading glance and she had to bite her lip to keep from laughing. She was darned if she was going to rescue him. It was high time for him to experience parenting. Sure enough, one of the first things he would have to learn was how to put Kendall on pause.

In the meantime Jessica was still clinging to her like a lifeline as they moved closer to the family group. When Kendall turned to acknowledge their presence and stopped for a second, Daniel was quick to take advantage. "It sounds like a great trip, Kendall. Maybe tonight, before bed, you can tell me the rest of the details, but I want to say hi to Annie and Jessica, too."

As Daniel moved toward them, Jessica stepped even closer to her aunt, half burying her face in Annie's skirt. Daniel stooped down until he was at eye level with the child. He obviously knew, without being told, that the younger twin wouldn't be as easy to win over as her sister.

He gave Jessica a moment to gather the courage to let go of Annie's hand and look him in the eye. Then he spoke. "Hi, Jessica. I hope that you can tell me something about the trip, too. But right now, how about if we all go out? Annie said something about getting you some winter coats."

She watched him in silence.

"Then maybe tomorrow we could go to Rockefeller Center and try some ice-skating."

To Annie's surprise, Jessica answered him: "I don't wanna skate. I only wanna watch."

He nodded. "Okay. Maybe I'll watch with you."

Jessica looked up at Annie and stepped back next to her without answering her father.

Daniel stood up, patted her on the head and faced Annie. He continued to smile, but his eyes hardened slightly. He pulled Annie into his arms and gave her a hug that took her breath away. It wasn't the force of the hug that left her breathless. It was the magnetism that drew her to him, the unexpected attraction that was unwelcome and unwanted.

Daniel released her slightly and smiled into her eyes. It was the same smile her friends had thought so appealing all those years ago; the same smile she'd labeled cynical.

"Annie you're as lovely as ever. It's great to see you."

Then he kissed her.

It was just a little kiss. Really, just a "kissin' cousin" sort of kiss, but so totally without warning. His lips settled warmly on hers for a moment. The soft caress of mouth, the woodsy scent of his aftershave, the press of his body against her, reminded Annie of every one of her private fantasies. Before awareness became response it was over. She was out of his arms and he was turning his attention to Kendall.

Whatever had gotten into him? she wondered. It was so out of character. Surely, he'd only done it to make the girls feel comfortable. But that token kiss had generated a whole charge of feelings that Annie would just as soon not think about, much less deal with.

She wanted to rub the tingling sensation off her mouth. She wanted to forget the feel of her body pressed against his. She wanted to dispel the unease that invaded her senses and cling to the animosity that she'd harbored for so long.

While Annie struggled to recover her equanimity, the twins put on their well-worn coats. Kendall explained that Annie had tried to order new coats from a catalog, but they'd sent the wrong size.

Annie turned to the mirror behind the bar on the pretext of adjusting her hat. She looked normal, thank God for that. With a deep steadying breath, she turned back to the group and prayed that Daniel would keep his distance.

The four of them trooped from the room, Annie bringing up the rear. She stuffed the key into her purse and shut off the lights as she listened to Daniel respond to one of Kendall's questions. Annie smiled at the threesome as they walked toward the elevator. Even in last year's too-small coats, the girls looked angelic. Kendall greeted a couple who were already waiting for the elevator. With Kendall around, they never had to worry about any uncomfortable silences.

By the time they reached the street, Kendall had begun to wind down and Jessica had relaxed enough to skip a little behind her sister, who was leading the way despite the fact she had no idea where they were going.

"It's hard to believe they're twins, isn't it?" Daniel spoke to Annie, but all his concentration was on the twosome ahead of him. "I mean, their personalities are so different."

"I know, I know. Most people don't even realize they're identical. Even standing still you can tell them apart. Kendall almost explodes with energy and Jessica, she's usually the picture of serenity."

Annie felt a measure of normalcy return. Things would be fine if they talked about the girls. Affection for them was the one thing—about the only thing—they had in common.

As they got closer to Fifth Avenue, Daniel suggested they take a cab. "It's really too cold for them to walk around in those lightweight coats. What do you think?"

It was a rhetorical question. Daniel had already stepped off the curb to hail a taxi. Annie nodded her agreement anyway and brushed aside the feeling that he was criticizing her because the twins were growing like normal children.

Fifteen minutes later they were in Macy's headed for the children's department. Even though it was close to Christmas, the store wasn't crowded once they got beyond the first floor. Counting their blessings, Annie made short work of picking out moderately priced snowsuits for the girls. It was Daniel who insisted that they buy dress coats, as well, and then added warm fur-lined boots.

As the pile of clothing grew, the girls' enthusiasm lessened. Annie was puzzled. Normally they enjoyed shopping, even though their endurance level was significantly less than an adult's. While Daniel was paying for the purchases, the girls donned their new coats and boots. It was Kendall who explained their concern in a whisper that somehow carried through the whole department, "Annie, do you think we'll still get toys for Christmas, too?"

Annie knew Daniel must have heard. *If you laugh, Daniel Marshall, I swear I'll murder you on the spot.*

Daniel didn't say a word. He arranged to have the package of snowsuits delivered to the hotel, then herded the group into the elevator and headed for the eighth floor. When three pairs of eyes turned to him in question, he smiled. "You know, Santa Claus puts in a little time here every day and I thought it would be a great idea for the two of you to sit on his lap and tell him what you want for Christmas." He glanced at Annie. "While you're doing that, Annie can sit on my lap." The girls giggled and Annie shook her head, smiling in spite of herself.

The four of them moved through the maze that wound through Santaland. The long line moved fairly quickly at first, allowing them only quick glances at the first scenes. Then the line slowed and they all watched the automated figures, marveling at the vignettes, enjoying the music.

Daniel and Annie stood off to one side while the girls waited in the final line to have their picture taken with Santa. Daniel turned his attention to Annie. "Speaking of Santa Claus, this Santa wants to know if you've taken care of the gifts yet."

Annie felt her defenses rising. The cynicism in his voice overrode the seemingly good-natured smile. "Yes, I did. I can show you a list and I have all the receipts. I have the packages in the closet in my bedroom. And listen, I'd better tell you, I bought a few things for myself—from Santa you understand—and even one or two things for you."

Daniel patted her shoulder in imitation of Santa seated a few feet away. "Of course. I'm sure you've been a good little girl, too. And money was no problem, either—was it?"

She knew he was referring to the blank check and once again her defenses rose, settling firmly in place. "Well, actually, it *is* fun to go out and play Santa Claus for yourself, especially with someone else's money."

Turning her back on him, she stepped away, willing an end to the interchange. She needed a moment to dispel the welter of emotions that kept her on edge. All her good humor had evaporated, to be replaced by a sharp awareness that was irritating and unwelcome.

As the girls walked over to them, Daniel stepped close once again. He finished the conversation by whispering in her ear, "I can hardly wait to see what you got me—something sentimental like itching powder or something pointed like a one-way ticket back to Africa?''

Annie whirled to face him, her face very close to his. She ignored the warmth of his eyes, the fan of his breath on her cheek. ''Daniel, you were easy to buy for, a lump of coal—gift wrapped.''

Daniel crossed to the cash register, smiling, and paid for the pictures. The foursome headed down the escalator and out into the cold December air. As the silence between them lengthened, Kendall filled the void. ''Annie, I told Santa about the new pen you want for your calligraphy and about the slippers, too.'' She turned to her father. ''Daddy, how come grown-ups don't talk to Santa Claus? How does he know what you want? I didn't know what you wanted, so I couldn't tell him.''

Daniel bent down to answer. ''Honey, the truth is, I don't need any more presents. You and Jessica are the best Christmas present I could have. I've been asking for it for quite a while. It's just taken a couple of years for me to get my wish.''

As they piled into the cab that conveniently discharged a passenger right where they were standing, Annie considered that last statement. The man was impossible to understand. He treated his children with love. He was obviously proud of them. If they meant that much to him, why hadn't he ever sent Kathy anything more personal than a child-support check? Why had he let years go by and then only come home when he found out that his ex-wife had been killed? He'd been writing to the children for months now; but it had been two years since the accident and he was only here now because Annie had pressured him into it.

He'd once been family, but all that had been lost when he left the country. Yet, spending a few hours with him today, she'd seen an occasional glimpse of the man she'd once found likable. One thing was certain; Daniel Marshall still incited the same sweep of emotions within her that he always had. One might even say that sweep had expanded some. Once it ranged from dislike to friendship. Now it went one step beyond friendship to awareness. Annie was honest enough to acknowledge it, but didn't want to accept it. Instead, she attributed it to Daniel's unexpected behavior. He seemed to have forgotten that they'd been friends, yet he'd kissed her when no such gesture had been necessary.

He was a puzzle, all right—one she had ten days to solve.

Chapter Two

Daniel threaded his way through the crowds pressed around the railing above the sunken ice rink hoping he could spot Annie and the girls without too much trouble. He glanced at the lighted tree crowning the rink that was the focal point of Rockefeller Center. Tree lights and decorations were lit despite the daylight, and the glitter was overwhelming.

Just as he maneuvered his way to a coveted spot by the railing, the sound system came to life and the strains of "White Christmas" poured into the air. Daniel groaned at the sensory overload. At the moment he felt more like Ebenezer Scrooge than Bing Crosby. He was late, the crowds formidable and the skies threatening rain.

He leaned forward, trying to make out individuals in the swirling mass of people below. Cameras clicked to his right and left, and more than one person commented on the press of skaters making their way around the oval surface.

The rink was crowded, but he didn't see his children or Annie. Actually, there were very few youngsters on the ice.

This morning, when they'd agreed to meet here, he hadn't anticipated that his appointment would run late. Was it too much to hope that they would still be waiting for him? Could they have gone back to the hotel already?

Being late certainly wouldn't impress Annie. It would be just one more entry on her black list. So what? he chided himself, ignoring the gut feeling that it *did* matter. This wasn't a popularity contest—at least not with Annie. What was one more mark added to a list six years long?

It was the twins that mattered. They seemed happy, even glad to see him. This was quite a change from the last time he'd seen them, when he'd come home for their mother's funeral. Then they'd treated him like the stranger he was. Could it be that a simple exchange of letters and pictures had made such a difference? Children were amazingly resilient, he decided.

The rink was surrounded by a restaurant with windows that looked out on the ice. On a hunch, he made a quick survey of the tables. Halfway around he spotted silver-blond hair and bright blue coats. He hurried to the entrance, elbowing his way through the crowd, as if shaving a few minutes off his tardiness would save him from criticism.

He could see them as he made his way through the restaurant. Kendall was chattering away. Annie was listening, nodding occasionally with her arm around Jessica. The little girl leaned against Annie while she watched the skaters. Annie was as touching as any Madonna Daniel had ever seen, never mind that she wasn't the twins' biological mother.

Just watching the trio, he knew that Annie was their mother in every other sense of the word. He'd been wise to leave them in her care after Kathy's death. As much as he'd wanted to share their day-to-day lives, the political situation in his part of Africa had been too unpredictable. After a few months he'd given up hoping that a truce would be declared just to accommodate his parental wishes. He'd had to accept the fact that he couldn't be with the girls until his African project was finished. He wasn't selfish enough to put them into a potentially dangerous situation.

He couldn't bring his children with him and he wasn't able to abandon his project and come home. He had a contract. His first important contract. And he was determined to fulfill it and leave with the best recommendation possible. His family's future depended on it.

There had been another reason he'd asked Annie to act as guardian as well. The children had just suffered an incredible loss. He could still remember how confused and lost they'd looked. He'd wanted to comfort them, but he was a stranger—a stranger suffering his own pangs of guilt and failure. He hadn't been much help at all. They needed the security of a familiar life-style while they grieved. They needed family and family was the cornerstone of the VerHollans' life.

With Kathy's death, the close-knit clan had gathered together to share their grief. More than once he'd heard someone tearfully comment, "Those precious girls are all you have left of Kathy." He'd watched it all from the outside. That was nothing new. From the beginning the VerHollans had excluded him, never making him feel any better than an interloper.

They hadn't known what to say when he'd asked if Annie would act as the girls' guardian. It was as though they didn't believe he was capable of understanding what it would mean to take the children away with their loss so fresh.

He'd understood, all right. He, more than anyone, knew how empty life was without Kendall and Jessica. But the bottom line was that he wanted to do what was best for his kids. That meant leaving them in Georgia until they adjusted to their loss, until they would welcome him as part of their lives. Annie was the natural choice. At one time they'd been friends. Even at the funeral, she'd done her best to include him, clearly embarrassed by her parents' cold shoulder.

He wondered if Annie had any idea how well her million-dollar ultimatum had fit in with his plans. This Christmas holiday was his chance to become a real person to them, to put a face to the man who'd been writing to them since their mother died. He hoped it wasn't too late.

The three of them were so engrossed in the view that they didn't see him. They were laughing and pointing out one of the skater's clown acts, an act that masked a very talented performer. He tapped Annie on the shoulder.

"Daddy, Daddy!" Daniel pulled out his seat to a chorus of greeting. They didn't seem annoyed, just glad to see him.

He turned to Annie, an apology forming, but she stopped him with a raised hand. Her smile surprised him. "I'm so glad you found us. I watched the rink entrance for a while, but we were late too and I was afraid maybe we'd missed each other. I was trying to decide what to do."

He pulled out the chair across from her and sat down. The twins' good humor echoed Annie's. Ebenezer Scrooge disappeared. All of a sudden, he felt more like Father Christmas. "Trouble getting a taxi?"

She nodded. "Is it some kind of conspiracy? All *you* have to do is step to the corner and suddenly one materializes. When I want one it seems every cabdriver's decided to go to Brooklyn and look for fares."

Daniel nodded sympathetically. "The truth is, I'm glad you couldn't get one. I know that's selfish, but I much prefer the smile you're wearing to the tongue-lashing I would have gotten if I'd kept you waiting too long. I'd forgotten how slow-moving global bureaucracy is. It's a tribute to New York's influence that the darn meetings even start on time."

Annie's smile faded and the two stared at each other. Daniel read attraction quickly followed by confusion, even anger. He understood. He'd felt the same flash of awareness and the same denial. With a deliberate effort, he turned to the children, "I thought I'd see the three of you out on the ice."

Jessica shook her head vigorously. "Annie wanted us to, but Kendall and I would just rather watch." She paused a moment and looked at the rink beyond the plate-glass window. "It looks really hard."

Daniel agreed with the twins. "That is a pretty experienced group out there. How about if I take you to the rink in Central Park? It's not as crowded and it would be a good place to learn. Then, when you feel more confident, we could come back here."

Before they could respond, a waiter approached and handed him a menu. Daniel looked at his daughters. "Well, what meal is this? It's a little late for lunch and too early for dinner."

"I'm having a hot fudge sundae and Jessica's having a dish of chocolate ice cream with marshmallow sauce."

Daniel nodded thoughtfully at them and turned to Annie. "And you?"

She smiled back, a mischievous smile that drew one from him. "Tea and a piece of that fabulous Black Forest cake on the dessert cart."

He looked up from the menu. "Black Forest cake? Still can't resist chocolate, huh?"

Annie leaned a little closer to him. "Aren't vacations wonderful?"

He slapped the menu closed and handed it back to the waiter without taking his eyes from hers. "Black Forest cake sounds good to me, too."

Daniel picked up the thread of conversation. "Tell me. What do you think? Do you want to try skating before we leave New York?"

Kendall was enthusiastic at first. "Yes! Well, maybe. We don't get any practice at home. We almost never have ice."

At that, Jessica joined the conversation. "But we do get snow, sometimes."

Kendall nodded. "I remember when we werc three, we had snow that lasted all night. Mommy let us go out at midnight and build a snowman."

Daniel glanced at Annie who was smiling as she shook her head. "I keep telling her that she's heard that story so many times, she only thinks she remembers it."

"Yeah, I know what you mean. My brother," he turned toward the twins and included them in the conversation, "he's your Uncle Davis, insists that he remembers the year Roger Maris hit sixty-one home runs and I can't believe anyone still in diapers could recall it."

He turned to Annie. "You remember Davis?" At her nod he continued, "He's living in New York now."

She was surprised. "He's in the States?"

Daniel nodded and turned back to the girls. He pointed out two boys in their teens, skating with an older couple. "My grandmother used to bring me and my brother here to skate every year. She always said this was the way to start the Christmas season. That's one of the reasons I wanted to come here today—sort of a Marshall family tradition."

Kendall spoke up. "Honest, Daddy? Did she really take you skating, out on the ice?" The child looked at the crowded rink and back at Daniel. Her smile reminded him of Annie's.

"She sure did. You know, I pretty much grew up in Africa. But every Christmas my parents got so busy at the mission, they'd send us to New York to spend the holidays with our grandmother." Kendall looked impressed and turned back to the window as Jessica pointed out a father-and-son duo.

Daniel turned to Annie, whose face was a picture of comic skepticism. "Is this for real?"

When he nodded, Kendall prompted, "Tell us the rest."

He warmed to the story and embellished it with all the down-home flavor he was capable of. The VerHollans weren't the only ones with a close family and shared traditions. "Then Granny got a little too frail and she would sit in here and order hot chocolate for us. We spent so long on the ice that by the time we came in, the cocoa was cold. It still tasted great."

He glanced at Annie. She looked uncertain, as though she suspected he'd concocted an elaborate tall tale. Something that would compete effectively with VerHollan legend.

Daniel searched his memory for the rest of the story, determined to convince her that his story was as valid as any she'd heard in Avon.

"By the time we reached college, we were 'too old' to skate, but my parents were gone and Granny really needed us, we needed her. The skating part wasn't important anymore, it was being together that mattered. The three of us would sit here together and have tea...." Daniel's voice trailed off as he glanced around the room. Until he'd given voice to the story, he hadn't realized how important that tradition had been. It wasn't very often he shared his feelings. He waited for Annie to trample them.

Annie nodded, drawn into the tale. She looked around the room as if visualizing the group. "It's funny how much some traditions can mean to a family."

She'd so neatly pinpointed his own thoughts that he felt uncomfortable. She wasn't supposed to understand. She wasn't supposed to be sympathetic. "Yeah, Davis and I had a great time watching the skaters."

Annie laughed aloud. "I bet you loved it. Two college men ogling the co-eds while Granny acted the chaperon."

Daniel shook his head. "We had eyes only for Granny." He paused a moment. "We'd come back later and ogle the co-eds."

"And try to impress them with your figure eights?" Annie added.

He turned to look at her directly. "Whose story is this, anyway?" Annie shrugged away the question with a grin.

Daniel looked around the room. "Granny died twelve years ago and we stopped coming. It's real nostalgic to be back. They renovated this place a while ago, but memories don't fade that easily."

The girls were engrossed in the scene outside and Annie turned to Daniel. "A Marshall Christmas tradition, right on this spot. Hmm... And here I thought that Daniel Marshall arrived in Avon, Georgia, with no past at all."

"Let's face it, Annie, there's an awful lot you don't know about me."

"So, maybe you should fill in some of the gaps." There was no challenge in her voice, just sincere interest. Annie sat with her back to the window, her head bent to the side as if it would improve her hearing. He had her undivided attention.

He tried to second-guess her reasons for the friendly overture. Maybe she was humoring him, or looking for some piece of his past that she could use against him. Or was the kindness she showed the twins an inherent part of her adult personality? No matter what her reasons, this was the closest she'd come to an olive branch and he grabbed it. He was going to be spending the next ten days with Annie. The whole experience would be a lot more pleasant if they both took a stab at mending fences. He only hoped it would be worth the effort.

"You want the story of my life? What would you like to know?"

She shrugged again, looking a little self-conscious. "Were you born here in New York, I mean the City?"

He relaxed a tad and concentrated on the sound of her voice, all throaty and mellow. "Don't tell me you're one of those people who think New York City is all there is to the state?"

"Not me." The response came so fast that Daniel knew he'd caught her in a fib.

"Both Davis and I were born in a little town upstate. My dad had a parish up there for a few years until he decided on missionary work."

"Your father really was a minister?" She sounded incredulous, as though she didn't understand how a God-fearing man could have spawned such a devil.

Daniel ignored the tone and answered, watching the dark blue eyes that reflected her feelings so clearly. "That's right. We left for Africa when I was seven and my folks lived there until they died. They never came back except for some fund-raising visits."

"How did you get your education?"

"My mother was a teacher and there were several scientists working nearby who got me interested in engineering. When I was ready for high school, I won a scholarship to the theological seminary in Virginia. I had a lot of catching up to do, especially in math, but I worked hard because by then I knew I wanted to be some kind of engineer."

"Wasn't it hard leaving your family?"

A typical VerHollan question. He didn't think any of them had left Avon since the day they were born. "Sure, but it was time to step out on my own. My folks always encouraged us to be independent, try new things. I was curious about life in the States. I hadn't lived in the U.S. for years."

Annie shook her head. "It's so different from the way I grew up. It's as though you're from another culture and happen to speak the same language."

Daniel laughed at that, watching the way her hair swung from side to side, framing her face in a honey-blond halo. "I wasn't even sure about that when I arrived in Georgia. At first that Southern drawl was as foreign to me as Russian would have been."

Annie laughed with him and deliberately thickened her slight accent. "Why, honey, we don't have any accent. It's y'all that talk different."

"That's what Kathy always used to say." He regretted the words immediately. At the mention of Kathy's name, the tension that had begun to dissipate materialized again. Two steps forward, one step back.

Daniel changed the subject, hoping to divert her thoughts, bring back her smile. "You know, I'd like to spend an evening with Davis while we're here."

It worked, but the residual bitterness tinged her words. "I'm really surprised that he came back to New York. I thought he'd decided to stay in Europe. How long has he been here? The girls have only met him a couple times. It would have been nice to invite him for a visit. Family is so important."

Daniel had to make a concentrated effort not to lash out at her. All these years the VerHollans had kept him from his children and here she was, mouthing how important family was. It wasn't something she had to tell him. He knew it as well as she did. He'd known it from the beginning.

The waiter arrived with their order and soon the table was covered with sweets. Daniel watched as the others reached for their spoons. Kendall started with the cherry and the biggest scoop of whipped cream, fudge and ice cream she could manage. Jessica took delicate little tastes and savored each mouthful. Then he turned to Annie. Her dessert forgotten, she was watching him watch Kendall and Jessica, her interest a question. He turned back to the children without comment. Daniel looked at the size of the servings and then at Jessica. "Are you going to be able to finish all that?"

"I don't know, but I'll try, 'cause I don't want to disappoint the cook."

Daniel thought the comment odd until Kendall chimed in, "Uh-huh, Annie gets real mad when Roy comes over and then complains about what she makes. Miss Winston says that you can't disappoint the cook and you gotta try everything, even if you don't think you'll like it."

Daniel looked questioningly at Annie, who defended herself. "The man has no sense of adventure. You'd think I'd served him sushi. If it's anything but fried chicken or steak, he complains." She stopped abruptly. "But surely, you don't want to hear about our little rural disappointments.

"No, I'm intrigued. It seems to be the day for revelations. Let me in on the secret. You have..." He leaned a little closer, "Tell me, exactly how would you describe this Roy?" His voice reflected the vividness of his imagination.

While Annie hesitated, Kendall answered for her. "He could be Annie's boyfriend. He's the gym teacher at school. He's gonna be our gym teacher next year. And Miss Winston's gonna be our classroom teacher."

The name Winston rang a bell, but Daniel had never heard of Roy. He envisioned a muscle-bound jock, one who drove a beat-up car or, better yet, a pickup with a gun rack in the rear, the sort of guy he personally couldn't stand.

Annie patted Kendall's hand and interrupted. "He's my boyfriend just like Mary Jane Winston's my girlfriend. We spend some of our free time together, that's all. He enjoys the girls and—"

Jessica decided to add her opinion. "He told me he wanted to get married to a beautiful blonde." Then she giggled. "And I'm not old enough to get married yet."

Daniel turned to Annie and raised his eyebrows, encouraging her comment. At that moment Jessica upset the cream pitcher as she reached for her water glass. Annie moved quickly to pick up the miniature pitcher and only a little of the liquid spilled on the tablecloth. She smiled at the child, who was about to cry. "Aren't we lucky that it's white? Look, Jessica, you can't even tell it spilled, especially if we put the sugar bowl on top of the spot."

Jessica's twin chimed in, "Oh, look at that beautiful lady skater. Isn't her green outfit pretty? Wow." The tears were averted and the two children were once again absorbed in the scene outside.

When the snack was over, Annie suggested that they visit the ladies' room before leaving. Daniel stood as they left. He resumed his seat in slow motion, intrigued by that bit of conversation about Roy.

So there was a man in her life. Maybe that explained her sudden desire to have his daughters get to know him. Maybe she was ready to settle down with Roy of the chicken-fried steak, and the girls would be in the way.

If that was the case, then her idiotic gesture with the check was easily explained. Maybe reclaiming custody of his children wouldn't be nearly as traumatic as he thought.

He wanted them with him. If he'd been unsure before, the last twenty-four hours had thoroughly convinced him how much he needed them. Kendall's enthusiasm and Jessica's serenity had already softened his outlook, had him looking at the world from a different perspective.

Where once New York seemed crowded and dirty, he now saw little details that made it magical in his children's eyes. The Christmas season and the city's excitement were fresh and new to them. Santa Claus and store windows, elevators and taxicabs, even Don't Walk signs, were an adventure.

Where once the world had seemed tired and doomed, he had only to look at Kendall and Jessica to see hope for the future. God, how he hoped his children needed him as much as he needed them!

He watched as Annie and the girls walked back through the crowded restaurant. The threesome did make a charming picture. The angelic trio attracted a good deal of attention as they paraded through the room. The girls were well mannered and Annie was full of life and good humor.

Annie paused as an elderly couple spoke to them, and Daniel watched her as she answered the couple. Twenty-four years old and unmarried. It was difficult to believe that she was still as sweetly innocent as she looked. What if it was all an act to convince him that it was time he took a stint at parenting so she could get on with her life? Wouldn't she be surprised when she found out that was exactly what he had in mind?

He tossed his napkin on the table and counted out the tip. Maybe a few direct questions would give him some answers.

Annie wondered what could possibly have happened in the ten minutes she'd been gone to destroy the tenuous truce that had developed over the last hour. She was three tables away and his ill humor was sending shock waves out to meet her. Good heavens, the man was a puzzle. Just when she thought she'd broken through that cynical, tough exterior he seemed to reserve just for her, he slipped right back into character. Was he already tired of playing Papa? Had he remembered an important meeting he'd missed? Or was he a misanthropic jerk who couldn't relax and enjoy himself? A sense of frustration welled up inside her. Why were some people so hard to reach?

She turned to the girls who were standing nearby, hats and coats on. "Why don't you go out by the rink, right where I can see you? We'll be there in five minutes."

Annie returned to the table and sat down while Daniel finished paying the bill. He sat back and gave her his full attention. With an acknowledging nod, he smiled slightly and returned her steady look.

They were all ready to leave and he was sitting there glaring at her. She couldn't decipher exactly what those eyes were communicating. His expression now wasn't nearly as friendly as the looks he gave his children. It was more speculative, as though he was trying to figure her out. What was there to figure out? She'd never been anything but honest with him. Annie wished he'd been as straightforward with her.

Didn't this man have any manners at all? Her disappointment gave way to a slow burn that was rare and dangerous.

She folded her hands demurely on the table in front of her and shook her head. She tried to smile, but anger was too close to the surface. "You *are* a puzzle, Daniel Marshall. I've had a very nice hour. And now it seems to me you're doing your best to spoil it. And I can't understand why." She stopped, waiting for him to speak.

He let her flounder, not helping at all. Now she watched him raise his eyebrows at her direct words. He folded his arms and leaned back a little further in his chair. "Tell me, Annie, exactly what are you looking for?"

She was surprised, puzzled, by the question. She wasn't looking for anything. "I just want you to see what wonderful children your little girls are."

If a nod could be cynical, his was. "That's what I thought you'd say, but I don't quite think it's the whole truth." He leaned forward, accusing, "What's the point in having them get to know me? What's in it for you?"

Annie leaned across the table. Anger made her voice intense. "Daniel, I can't begin to explain 'what's in it for me,' as you put it. The point is, you're their father and they're reaching an age when having a father—at least knowing who he is—is important to them. If you don't intend to come home and be their father, then the least you can do is visit occasionally.

"The fact is, Daniel, the only two people who are enjoying this experience are outside watching the skaters. But frankly, that's enough for me. The fact that you find it a bore and won't look at it from their point of view only reaffirms my opinion of you."

Annie stood up and took a deep breath to control the anger pulsing through her. She turned to leave and then spoke to Daniel over her shoulder, "We're walking back to the hotel. I suppose we'll have to see you later."

She hurried out of the restaurant. Right now the company of a thousand surly New York pedestrians was preferable to his.

Chapter Three

Daniel walked home with them despite Annie's obvious inclination to be alone. As they entered the hotel, the girls raced ahead to push the button for the elevator. Annie sighed and hung on to the illusion of normalcy they presented. Anyone watching would assume they were a family—mother, father and two daughters caught up in the holiday spirit. She hoped no one could sense the tension that radiated between the two adults.

It was so disappointing. During the holiday season everyone should be at peace. She didn't understand his anger, anyway. What did he think she wanted? She supposed that the little game with the check and its million-dollar demand may have confused him. Didn't he realize that she'd only sent the blasted check to get his attention? Hadn't she made it clear that money wasn't what she was looking for?

They were on the elevator now, Kendall chattering away. She watched Daniel as he tried to answer one question before she asked another. As they walked down the hall toward their suite, he looked distracted, but intent on giving his daughter the attention she demanded.

You would think he'd be grateful, Annie thought. Instead, he treated her, his children's guardian, with a mixture of tolerant disdain and patronizing amusement. Once or twice there had been something else, a nameless communication that didn't have anything to do with the children. She did her best to ignore those looks and the feelings they generated. She pretended they were the look of a man trying to solve a complicated riddle. The real clue lay in the fact that she didn't believe in playing games. She was as straightforward and honest as she knew how. When he figured that out, maybe they could move beyond antipathy to something closer to a truce.

Daniel held Jessica's hand while Kendall ran ahead with the key. He was the puzzle. He seemed to know what each child needed, showing a sensitivity at odds with his long-term behavior. If he'd ever shown any interest in the girls before she'd pressured him into it, she would feel more tolerant now. But she couldn't forget—or forgive—all those months, years, when Kathy waited for the mail. Of course, he'd always sent the child support. The check was always there, usually early, never late, but never a letter, no pictures for the children.

All those years lost. Even if the marriage had ended, why did he have to deny the girls any contact? Was it his way of extracting revenge? Didn't he realize that he lost as much as the children did?

Maybe he was realizing it now. Maybe all this anger at her was misdirected. Was it possible Daniel felt guilty, too? Could it be that he was thinking about what might have been?

The suite had been made up while they were gone. Kendall and Jessica were impressed, racing from room to room to see if the beds were indeed made and all the dishes removed. Daniel turned to Annie and they smiled at each other, drawn together for a moment by the girls' naiveté.

"Daddy, Daddy, can you play a game with us?" Kendall pulled her father toward the living room.

He pulled back. "I'll tell you what. You two come to my room. I have a little something that might make it easier to wait for Christmas."

He didn't include Annie in the invitation, so she made herself busy straightening the coats. She slipped into her room and sat on the edge of the bed.

Picking up the phone, she punched out the numbers that would connect her with her parents in Avon. She'd promised to call every other day. Annie knew how lonely this Christmas was going to be for them.

"Hello." The sweet, velvet-coated voice of Lillian VerHollan echoed over the long-distance line.

"Hi, Mother. It's Annie." Annie knew better than to try and squeeze in any more. Her mother launched into conversation like a rocket soaring through the upper reaches of the atmosphere.

"Why, Annie, honey, we've been waitin' for your call. We're supposed to go over to the Bennetts' this afternoon, but I told your father I wasn't leaving this house until I heard from you. I wished you'd called yesterday—never mind that every-other-day nonsense. You can call collect, we can certainly afford a little bigger phone bill. I was worried that maybe something happened to you. But Wallace said that was nonsense. They service those airplanes all the time. Still then, I didn't know what would happen once you got to that awful city. He said you were just being independent, no matter that it hurt our feelings and we were worried sick...."

Annie flopped back on the bed. No question where Kendall got her nonstop conversational style from. As for "worried sick," her mother worried when Annie went to

Augusta, much less New York City. Thank goodness her father was around to appease her.

She kept tabs of the conversation from habit and waited for a pause.

"Is that man there yet?"

Annie sat upright and prayed for inspiration. "Yes, Mother, Daniel's with the girls now."

"Do you think he should be alone with them?"

Annie rolled her eyes, grateful that her mother wasn't any closer than the long-distance connection. It flashed through her mind that Daniel had been doing them all a favor when he insisted on New York as their meeting point. "Mother, of course he should be alone with them. For goodness' sake, he's their father. He's supposed to be with them."

She could hear Daniel and the girls laughing and chattering in the other room. "Actually they seem to be having a good time together." *As long as I'm not around,* she added to herself.

"I want to talk to Kendall and Jessica."

"Mother, I already told you that they need this time to build a relationship with their father. All you'll do is distract them. They don't need that."

She closed her eyes and waited. *I'm sorry, Mama, but you've got to let go a little.*

"Well, I never. Then why did you call, if you're not going to let me talk to my babies?"

"They're your grandchildren, Mother, not your babies. I called to let you know that we got here all right. Tell Daddy I said hi, you hear?"

"Yes, I hear." Her voice carried the hard edge of anger. "I guess there's no point in continuing this conversation if you insist on being so difficult. I just might not be here the next time you call."

An idle threat, but Annie knew her mother well enough to hear the disappointment.

"Now, Mama, I love you and I love the girls and I'm only doing what's best for everyone."

"I'm sure you think so. I just don't know who appointed you right hand to the Almighty, Annie."

"Old argument, Mama." Her good humor was slipping away.

She heard her mother sigh and she tensed. She knew what was coming.

"Annie, I know you think you're doing what's right. And I know I'm not making it any easier. But I do miss them."

The tears in her voice played on Annie's uncertainty. "I know that, Mama. You can talk to them in a couple of days."

"I suppose that will have to do. You keep an eye on that Daniel Marshall. Don't let him kidnap those darlings."

Annie bit her lip to keep from laughing at the absurdity of Daniel kidnapping his own children. She mumbled "Goodbye" and hung up the phone.

Annie rubbed the back of her neck and reached into the drawer for some aspirin. She thought about calling Mary Jane. Her friend would give her the sympathetic ear her mother would not. Annie wouldn't have to pretend a conviction she didn't feel. Mary Jane understood how ambivalent her feelings about Daniel were and agreed that she was doing the right thing in trying to involve him in his children's lives. When her mother had cried and begged her not to take Kendall and Jessica to meet their father, Mary Jane had agreed that Daniel deserved this Christmas. After all, he'd missed the last six.

She could tell Mary Jane that she and Daniel could hardly be civil to each other for more than an hour at a stretch. Mary Jane would understand that it was going to make for a very long visit and not much of a vacation.

There was a tap on the door just as she picked up the phone to dial the number.

"Annie, come look." It was Kendall, who waited until she opened the door, and then took her hand.

Spread out on the floor surrounded by a large box and quantities of packing straw was a dollhouse. African-style. It was a little village of three grasslike houses and seven little people in native costume. There were several animals carved from wood and painted in detail.

"Daddy made these for us. Look! The back of the house opens and you can make the people go inside." Kendall turned to her father. "Daddy, where do they put their cars?"

Daniel laughed and began to talk about the way the people in the villages lived. He used the dolls and animals to illustrate the story and Annie sat on the nearby love seat, as intrigued as the children.

Daddy made these for us. The project had obviously taken weeks of work. The suggestion of devoted father didn't jibe with her image of the man who'd sent a blank check to cover his daughters' Christmas and birthday presents.

"It's so hot that the natives think it's cold if the temperature falls below ninety degrees."

"Wow. Is that why they don't wear clothes?"

Jessica piped up. "How come they don't wear sunscreen? Annie makes us wear it so we don't get cancer." She looked at her aunt for approval and Annie smiled and nodded.

Daniel went on to explain about cancer and other diseases that the people faced, but countered it with stories about good times, too.

He was a natural with the children. After two days she was sure it wasn't an act. He obviously cared about them, loved them as only a father could. How could he spend this time with them and then go back to Africa? How could he get to know them, see how wonderful they were and then abandon them again?

Exactly what were his plans? It was pointless to speculate. She'd never been able to figure him out before. This time she didn't have to try. He was right here, next to her. All she had to do was ask.

It was a pretty room. More than that, it was comfortable, despite its hotel-like perfection. It would be the ideal spot for a romantic evening for two. Annie turned the lights up higher. Romance was not what was on her mind. She looked around once again, eyeing the powder-blue love seats set at right angles to each other, one of them parallel to the fireplace. It could even be an effective business environment. A large square coffee table separated the love seats from two wing chairs in a blue-and-rust floral pattern. The whole was bound together by an elegant Oriental carpet that echoed the color scheme.

The coffee table was just big enough for the African village still spread on the surface, though a bowl of flowers would probably be more in keeping with the elegant atmosphere. Maybe she would buy a Christmas arrangement tomorrow—that is, if Daniel didn't think the expense too frivolous.

Annie walked over to the fireplace contemplating a dozen ways to avoid spending any time with him tonight. As much as she wanted to stage a strategic retreat to her own room, there were subjects they had to discuss, decisions to be made. Procrastinating would only prolong the strain. And her near-constant headache indicated that the state of tension could only increase so much before she lost her composure altogether.

There was a packet of instructions written on an elegant card resting on the mantel. Annie read carefully, turned the key and touched a match to the logs in the fireplace. With a gentle whoosh the gas ignited and the flames flickered through the logs in a credible imitation of a wood fire. She adjusted the control, reducing the gas flow, and stood up.

She stared into the flames, thinking about the last few hours and how much Daniel seemed to enjoy the simple domestic routine, playing with Kendall and Jessica, watching the rerun of some animated Christmas special and eating supper. A few moments ago he'd tucked the children in with hugs and kisses. It was the same routine she always found rewarding. Apparently that was one thing they agreed upon.

They'd discussed some of their vacation plans at dinner. The girls were anxious to learn to skate and interested in the Christmas show at the Hayden Planetarium.

Daniel had even arranged a dinner with his brother. They all were looking forward to that. She thought of the few times she'd met Davis Marshall. She didn't know him well, just enough to appreciate his carefree, vagabond nature. She remembered how much the twins had enjoyed his elaborate games of make-believe.

The girls hadn't been quite as enthusiastic about the Museum of Natural History or even Radio City Music Hall until she explained about the Rockettes. They hadn't talked about Christmas Eve plans yet. Annie wondered if Daniel felt attending a church service was as important as she did. Or had he left his religious faith behind?

She could hear the murmur of voices in the other room, and recognized the script of a hundred questions Kendall used regularly when she wanted to delay bedtime.

Annie sat on the floor and fingered the African village scene that had held the girls' attention all evening. She tucked the baby doll into the hut and sat the mother figure next to the father and imagined them staring into the make-believe fire the girls had made from packing straw. Even in Africa people must have trouble communicating. Even in Africa different families must have different value systems. Did they make it work any better than Americans did?

Annie leaned her head back against the foot of the couch and closed her eyes, trying to erase her headache by concentrating on the positive. It was Christmas, the children were with their father, the three of them—

"Annie, tell me, what's the secret? How do you get Kendall to be quiet long enough to fall asleep?"

Caught by surprise, Annie jerked up, dropping the doll she'd been holding. Daniel moved into the room, toward the love seat opposite her, and sat down.

Annie made herself relax, urging the tension out of her shoulders. She concentrated on answering his question, trying for the same friendly tone he'd used.

"Actually, Jessica's the one who clued me in. Kendall doesn't talk without an audience. Jessica says if you pretend you're asleep, then Kendall stops talking."

Daniel nodded and the silence between them lengthened. Daniel leaned back into the cushions taking small sips from a glass of brandy.

Annie watched a moment, desperate for something to say. "You used to smoke a pipe, didn't you?"

"Yeah, I left it behind by mistake and decided this was as good a time as any to quit. Now *that* was a dumb idea."

It was the first time Annie had heard him admit that he found the tension as uncomfortable as she did. She watched him for a moment as he stared at his glass of brandy. What in the world could they talk about? Was now the time to ask about his future plans?

It seemed Daniel had an agenda of his own. "You might have made a mess of my accounting, Annie, but you really did me a favor when you tried to cash that check for a million dollars."

Not that again, Annie moaned. It was the third time he'd brought the subject up. Never once had he accepted her explanation or even taken the time to listen to it. Besides *he* was the one who'd sent the blank check. Let's see how he felt on the defensive. "How about if you tell me why you sent the check in the first place? It was a pretty callous thing to do. This from a man who says he cares about his children?"

Daniel nodded as though it were a reasonable request and not an attempt to goad him. "You know about the civil war in the region?"

Annie nodded.

"Right about the time I sent the check, I thought there was a good chance our project area was going to come under fire and a distinct possibility that the Americans there would be taken hostage."

All her anger evaporated. "Oh, Daniel, I had no idea. I mean, I knew about the fighting. It made the national news a few times." She didn't add that more than once, she'd worried about his safety. She would have been much more distraught if she'd known he was actually in danger.

It never occurred to her that her emotional reaction was inconsistent with her claim of intense dislike for him.

"I'd worked so hard at establishing communication with the children. I was afraid of what would happen if I suddenly stopped writing. I thought if I sent the check then, you could keep up appearances until the situation sorted itself out."

"Now that you explain it, the whole thing makes a lot more sense." The shock of his revelation had worn off. The whole mess could have been so easily avoided. The thought touched off a new spark of anger. "It would have helped if you'd given me a hint when you sent the check. Your note was so vague—well, maybe not exactly vague, but brusque. You're always so darn cryptic, Daniel. The whole thing's like a card game to you. And you think any real communication will give away your hand."

Annie leaned forward, her arms resting on the table. She wanted him to understand that there was a way for them to work together. "It shouldn't be like that, Daniel. Where those children are concerned we should be working together, like bridge partners, not poker players."

"That's nicely said, Annie, but what makes you so sure we have the same goal?" Daniel leaned back into the cushions once again and took a sip of brandy. "Exactly what message were you sending me when you filled that check out for a million dollars?"

She could tell his relaxed pose was just for show. She felt like a witness for the defense. And he was the prosecuting attorney just waiting for words he could use against her. "I told you this afternoon. I wanted to remind you that you have two daughters who need you more than they need your money."

He leaned forward. The illusion of relaxation was gone. He looked angry, as if his feelings were restrained behind a thin veneer of civility. "What makes you think that I forgot for one minute exactly what those children need? Who was I thinking of when I let them stay on with you in Avon after Kathy died? If I'd had my way, they would have been on the plane back to Africa with me."

Despite the anger, Annie relaxed a little. He might have done the right things then, but he'd made a few mistakes since. She picked up one of the dolls and straightened its clothes. She really didn't want to argue; this time she wanted some answers.

"I understand that. You said your contract only had one more year to run. But now one year's stretched to two. In all this time you never gave us any hint when you'd come back. What was I supposed to think? I've already told you I've never had much luck trying to guess your plans or your feelings."

The man really wouldn't give anything away. Did it all have to be dragged out of him? "Don't we both want what's best for Kendall and Jessica?"

"Ahh, but do we define that the same way?"

Annie played on, but she was getting increasingly tired of second-guessing his motivation. "I want you to be a part of their lives, a father in action and not just in name. I've said that dozens of times before."

He agreed and went on. "I'm not sure that when it comes to me 'being a part of their lives,' we'd agree on exactly what that means."

It was an issue she was willing to discuss, but he went on before she could speak.

"How would you feel if I told you that I plan to come back to the States?"

Surprise made her blunt. "Do you?"

"That's what these meetings are all about. If I do have to go back after Christmas it will only be for a few weeks."

Annie stifled the cynical smile, but the disbelief echoed in her words. "I've heard that before. You have the oddest calendar I know. Your idea of a few weeks would probably be another six months."

Now he was on the defensive. "Annie, the point is, this project involves years of work and millions of dollars. That water means life, and we aren't talking swimming pools and sprinkler systems. It means survival. I couldn't walk away from it. I wouldn't—not when we're so close to success."

"And now you're willing to risk it all?" She wasn't convinced that a man who'd abandoned his family for so long could change his priorities so easily.

"I've got a guarantee from both sides that the project is neutral territory. All I have to do is clear my stuff out and hire a permanent project coordinator, preferably someone local and acceptable to both sides.

"That's it. Then I'm coming home to be a father, to try and undo some of the damage done all these years."

"I'll believe it when I see it, Daniel. What's to keep you from finding another project that's more important than your family? Maybe it would make more sense if you would explain why in heaven's name you went to Africa in the first place."

The question didn't surprise him. The VerHollans weren't the type to forget the past. Annie might insist it would help her understand, but Daniel thought it only gave her more fuel for the resentment that had burned steadily since he and Kathy had married.

He was through with games. He owed her some answers, just as she owed him some understanding. Maybe being honest would get them both what they wanted. He looked at Annie and wished again for his pipe, even a cigarette, anything that would be some sort of shield. Being frank with her was more difficult than he'd imagined.

"You want to know why I went to Africa? The answer is simple. I went for the money." That was honest, if incomplete. He would wait and see exactly how much she wanted to hear.

"Oh, come on." She shook her head. "Sometimes I think you just want me to think the worst of you. Believe me, Daniel, you don't have to work at it. It comes naturally."

She paused a moment. Daniel thought maybe she'd decided against an inquisition.

She hadn't. "There must be more to it than that."

He conceded the point with a nod.

"So, why Africa?"

"When the girls were born, I was thrilled, the classic proud papa. Twins, no less. I was amazed." Daniel had her complete attention now and he went on, "But I was also unemployed."

He would have continued, but Annie interrupted. "But you'd just finished graduate school. Surely you realized it would take a while to find a job?"

"I'd been talking to recruiters for three months and believe me, Annie, there were no prospects. They only wanted people with degrees *and* practical experience. I'd been in school all my life. Experience was one thing I didn't have."

He sipped the brandy. Just talking about the events recalled the anxiety of those days, the tension that had taken away so much of the joy he'd felt as a new father.

"There I was, with a wife and two infant daughters, and no way to support them. Then after about five months of worry, I got a call from a contractor for AID, the Agency for International Development. They had a project in West Africa. Their head engineer had died of a heart attack, his assistant was moving up to head the program, but they needed a backup and they needed someone fast. A friend in the State Department recommended me."

He leaned forward in his seat. "It was a great opportunity, Annie. I knew a little about western Africa. The money was good. In fact, it was everything I'd hoped for. I went up to D.C., had the interview and signed the contract. Then I came back to tell Kathy."

He didn't add that he'd had other reasons for accepting the offer. He hadn't wanted to stay in Augusta and he *certainly* hadn't wanted to move to Avon. In fact, he'd been anxious to wean Kathy from a family he thought was overprotective, a family that had always viewed him as a threat. The circumstances of their marriage—the unplanned pregnancy—hadn't helped. It had only reinforced their perception of him as a man whose goal was to destroy their family. Almost from the start of Daniel's job search, Wallace VerHollan had pressured him to take a job with his firm so his daughter and granddaughters would be near.

Annie nodded. "I remember when you came back and were telling Daddy about it. It sounded like a greatest adventure in the world to me."

"It did?" He felt a mix of surprise and disbelief.

"For goodness' sake, Daniel. It wasn't like you didn't know what you were doing. I mean, you practically grew up in Africa, so it was sort of like going home."

She smiled for the first time that evening. "Do you remember the big Fourth of July celebration the year you all made the trek to Avon? I must have spent half the day telling Kathy everything I had read about that part of Africa."

It was news to Daniel. He remembered that weekend as a mass of dark looks and resentment. "I thought I was on your blacklist that weekend. I forgot the fireworks or some such thing."

Annie laughed. "You were. But Africa wasn't. Besides, Kathy would never let me bad-mouth you in those days." She bit her lip as though she regretted the last phrase and hurried on, "So, Daniel, why didn't you take Kathy with you?"

Daniel shook his head at the question. Before he could answer, he had to fight back a wave of bitterness. It was typical for a VerHollan to put the blame on his back. He narrowed his eyes and his reminiscent tone turned cynical. "Too bad you can't ask Kathy why she refused to come."

Annie straightened. "She refused to go with you?"

"Exactly."

Annie still looked uncertain. "Let me get this straight. You wanted to take Kathy and the children and she said no?"

"That's it. She told me that she wasn't taking her babies to some strange land, at least not until they finished their vaccinations. She kept saying she needed help, that she couldn't manage the twins alone. When I insisted we could have servants, she started talking about the baby we'd lost and how she couldn't face that pain again. Well, I understood that. I kept trying to tell her that there were perfectly capable doctors in Africa, but her mind was made up.

"Talk about a bind, I was stuck. I'd already signed the contract. I was committed, even if she wasn't. The truth is, it never even occurred to me that she wouldn't want to go."

Annie was still sitting ramrod straight, her expression puzzled.

Daniel sat back in his chair, tired of the continuing cross-examination. "Didn't you ever ask Kathy about this?"

Annie looked away and spoke slowly, as if she didn't want to voice the words. "She told me that you said maybe she and the twins could come later, but that you wanted to be on your own for the first few months."

Daniel sighed. Kathy's manipulation of the truth didn't surprise him a bit. "Sounds like two different stories, doesn't it?"

"But why would Kathy lie? She missed you, Daniel. She cried all the time at first."

Daniel had reached his limit. He stood up and moved from the intimacy of the fireplace setting. He paced away for a moment, then turned back. He knew why Kathy had lied. He knew why she'd cried, too. She'd wanted him back all right, but only on her own terms. She wanted him in Augusta, or better yet, in Avon where he would smother in the bosom of her family. Kathy had never understood that the four of them had become a family, that it had been time for her to grow up and make a home with him.

Daniel turned back to Annie one more time, leaning over the back of the couch he'd been sitting on. "Annie, Kathy didn't want to leave home. She couldn't make herself break away."

"But, Daniel, she'd just had a baby—twins. She wasn't ready for another big change."

He waved away her protest and decided to call it a night. Before he turned to his room Daniel spoke one more time. "Think about it, Annie. You all made it too easy for her to give up on our marriage. Did anyone ever tell her she should be with her husband?"

Annie sat still.

"God knows, it wasn't all your fault. I should have talked the whole idea over with her before I signed the contract. I should have figured out a way to postpone the trip instead of trying to talk her into joining me when I was already thousands of miles away. The list of 'shoulds' on my side is pretty long. But in the end, what chance did I have against a barrage of VerHollans that wouldn't let go?"

He closed his door quietly, leaving Annie alone with his last bitter words.

Chapter Four

Daddy's taking us skating, Annie." With a fine disregard for years of training, Kendall burst though the bedroom door without knocking.

Suppressing a groan, Annie turned to face the door. Before falling asleep she'd spent hours trying to come to terms with Daniel's story. Now Kendall had awakened her from a bizarre dream that seemed to be a subconscious replay of last night's conversation combined with surreal vignettes Annie couldn't quite recall.

Ice-skating? Had the child said ice-skating? "That's nice, honey. When are we leaving?" She was barely able to move yet, and tried to calculate how fast she could shower and dress.

"Daddy said he wants to take just us so you could have some time to yourself."

That was nice of Daniel, Annie thought, but she could hardly equate his altruism with his anger of the previous night. She'd fully expected him to ignore her this morning after the way he'd stormed out of the room. A dream fragment edged into her musings. He would ignore her until she begged for his attention. She shook away the absurdity. Now, where had that thought come from?

She wanted Daniel to pay attention to Kendall and Jessica, not to her. She only wanted his attention long enough to make him see that the girls were the most important part of his life.

A light tap on the door interrupted the ordering of her thoughts.

Kendall ran to answer it and Daniel entered the room carrying a tray, followed by Jessica bearing the newspaper.

He was smiling. It was a cautious smile as though he wasn't sure of her reaction. What was he worried about? She wasn't the one who'd gone off in a huff last night. She'd been fully prepared for ill humor, not for this tentative peace offering.

While Kendall propped up her pillows, Annie tried to keep both eyes open at the same time. She watched as Daniel slid the tray onto the dresser. He turned to face her and leaned against the edge. His smile had faded, but he was still silent. He stood across the room and watched her.

Annie opened her mouth, but swallowed her words in a huge yawn.

That seemed to tell Daniel everything he needed to know. He turned to the coffee service and poured a cup. "The girls *did* warn me. Not a morning person, I take it?"

His back was to her, but Annie could have sworn that now he was laughing. Daniel spoke with the superiority of someone who was up before the rooster, with half the day's work done before she'd had her first cup of coffee.

Annie struggled up a little higher on the pillows. "I've always thought if God had meant us to be up before noon, he would have made it one of the commandments. It goes against human nature to be cheerful before 8:00 a.m."

He approached the bed with a cup and a napkin. "Do you want some coffee?" His smile was a grin now—one that stopped short of a chuckle.

Daniel sat at the foot of the bed and instantly Annie was wide-awake and aware of exactly how unnerving his presence was. Her dreams may have been too vague to recall, but the emotions they'd generated made her uncomfortable, restless. Once again she forced her thoughts away from the pull of her dreams. It was simply inappropriate for Daniel to be in her bedroom. She could hear her mother chanting number two hundred fifty-three in what she and Kathy had called the Lady's Litany: One never remained alone in one's bedroom with a gentleman other than one's husband. But then she wasn't alone. Her two eight-year-old nieces made perfectly adequate chaperons.

"Girls?" Daniel's voice stopped the twins as they pirouetted around the room full of energy and excitement. "Do your dad a favor, and go stack up the cereal dishes, will you? Then pick out your warmest clothes. It's cold out there today."

As her two chaperons raced through the door, Annie sipped the coffee and decided that she was being entirely too Victorian. Hadn't she and her sister crossed off all but a handful of the litany? Her flannel nightgown was as conservative as a nun's and the thick layer of sheets and blankets would surely protect her from Daniel's X-ray vision.

Problem was, there was no protection from the way her imagination raced now that he was within touching range. The subconscious fantasy of the night before was still too near for her to be fully armored against him. The thought surprised her. Daniel? Why, he'd never made any intimate gesture toward her. In fact, beyond that first welcoming kiss, he'd barely touched her. Why should his presence send her thoughts rioting? She didn't even like him.

"So I thought I'd give you a chance to have breakfast in bed, finish your shopping, even go to a museum. The truth is, Annie, it's my way of saying I'm sorry about last night. I shouldn't have walked out. I should have stayed and finished the discussion. It's the only way we'll ever clear the air between us. Maybe if I'd spoken up before, we wouldn't be in this situation now. Instead, I've nursed my resentment and blamed it all on your family. I decided last night, or maybe it was this morning, that you and I can change that. The thing is, with those two so full of energy, it'll be a while before we have some time alone again."

He wasn't laughing now. He was dead serious and waiting for her response.

Her reaction was important to him and Annie knew it. She recognized the effort it took for him to apologize, the effort it took for him to open up and explain behavior that he'd never had to justify before. He'd made it clear last night that he thought he was the one who'd been wronged. Indeed, the way she heard it, he felt the VerHollans owed him an apology.

His words were an admission that any resolution would have to be a joint effort. He needed Annie's cooperation. From his carefully neutral expression, Annie realized he wasn't at all sure he was going to get it.

The solid wall of dislike cracked a bit. How could he doubt for a minute that she would be unwilling to overlook that burst of temper? There were hard feelings on both sides. Surely he was entitled to an occasional residual bitterness, just as she was inclined to question past motivation and future intent.

She cleared her throat and took a sip of the coffee. "I appreciate the gesture, Daniel, and the apology." She wasn't sure she was giving the right answer, but at least she was being truthful.

He nodded and his smile reappeared. He got up from the bed, walked to the door and then turned around. "We should be back after lunch. I'll leave the Do Not Disturb sign out so you can have some privacy."

Annie slipped down under the covers although sleep was the farthest thing from her mind. She would probably spend all morning thinking about what Daniel had just done. He'd opened up and shared. And it wasn't just experience he shared, but his feelings. A warm, wild excitement touched her heart. It was her first glimpse of what a truly wonderful person he could be. Annie wasn't sure whether the last few moments had been the key to a Pandora's box or a treasure chest.

As he was about to close the door, he stuck his head in once more. "How is it those flannel nightgowns can look so cute on the twins and so sexy on you?" He closed the door and left her to blush alone.

Annie rummaged through her purse and pulled out four quarters. With exact fare in hand, she hopped onto the M-2 bus as it headed down Fifth Avenue. She'd browsed through some of the smaller shops on Madison Avenue and then walked the long block to Fifth to catch the bus down to the larger department stores.

She hadn't been entirely sure of the correct direction, but people had proved surprisingly helpful, including reminders that she would need exact change for the bus fare. The magic of the holidays in New York seemed to infect everyone with the same goodwill. People smiled when she did, one man even tipped his hat. There were no seats on the bus, but no one appeared to mind. They all seemed to have visions of their personal sugarplums dancing in their heads.

As the bus inched down the grid-locked avenue, Annie eyed her fellow passengers and the pedestrians outside. Despite the numbers, the world passed by in pairs or in family groups and her enthusiasm waned. Even her busmates seemed to be traveling in twos except for a few elderly ladies who sat isolated, looking as lonely as she felt.

She was still suspicious enough of Daniel to wonder if he'd done it on purpose. Was it his way of giving her some idea of what it was like to be on the outside?

It wasn't much fun.

And he'd endured it for years.

Until last night she'd thought it had been his choice. Kathy had always spoken as if Daniel were the one who'd left, and like a loyal sister, Annie had accepted her story without question.

Now she wasn't so sure. Daniel's version made sense. If even one VerHollan had insisted Kathy's place was with him, Annie wouldn't feel so guilty now. But it hadn't been that way. Her family's willing acceptance of the separation had made Kathy's refusal to join Daniel easier and easier, until divorce seemed the next logical step.

And Daniel had been pushed to the outside of a family unit he'd helped to create. No wonder he was bitter. No wonder he resented the VerHollans.

Was he really serious about returning to the States? Would he really consider being a resident parent? In the midst of the crowded bus, a spiral of loneliness squeezed her heart. In a moment of complete honesty, Annie admitted that wasn't what she wanted at all.

She wanted the girls to know their father. She wanted him to be a part of their lives. But she wasn't totally altruistic. For years she'd condemned her parents' possessiveness, but now Annie realized just how much of a VerHollan she was. She didn't want to give the girls up. They could visit Daniel for a week here and there, maybe even a month or so as they grew older, but could she say goodbye and be nothing more than an occasional visitor?

The conflict of emotion brought her close to tears. Her million-dollar demand had taken the situation out of her hands. For the first time she wondered if she'd started something that might end far differently than she'd imagined. Impatient with the slow-moving bus and her own depressing thoughts, Annie exited at the next stop.

It was Christmas—no time to dwell on those negative scenarios. Now was the time for pleasures, both real and imagined. The stately splendor of Tiffany's beckoned and with a shrug she decided to treat herself to an imaginary Christmas present.

The store was crowded with holiday shoppers and a few tourists like herself. Even full of people, the store had a hushed grandeur, almost like a church. The analogy conjured up all sorts of unkind thoughts about man and his materialistic tendencies, but Annie quashed them all. She blithely convinced herself that each shopper was just like her, impressed with the beauty of the jewels and not something as mundane as their value.

Patiently working her way through the crowds at the entrance, she stepped deeper in the store and found a spot at the first empty counter. The case contained enamel jewelry, some inlaid with semiprecious stones. The settings were fabulous and Annie wanted to know more about them. It was difficult to tell what the stones were and whether the pieces were one of a kind or not. She looked for a clerk, but all the salespeople were busy, the muted hum of conversation interrupted intermittently by the sound of clerks rapping on the glass counters.

She wanted to ask someone what the noise meant, but Kendall wasn't there to interrupt the nearest stranger. She wanted to share her pleasure in the jewelry, but Jessica wasn't there to exclaim over the colors with her. She wanted to trade pretend gifts with someone, but she was alone.

Daniel had promised her the whole morning, but she'd had enough. She looked around for a clock and moved toward the doors. Whether it was noon or not, Annie was determined to find a cab and head back to the hotel.

If Daniel had felt the way she did now, how had he endured years away from his children? Magnify her twinge of loneliness tenfold and it would be unbearable. Had he thought of them as often as she did? Had he wanted to share things with them that were now lost forever?

Maybe he really did mean to come home. His project was almost completed; only paperwork remained. If he had to go back, he claimed it would only be for a little while.

What if he came back and claimed his rightful custody of the girls? What were the chances he would settle anywhere near Avon, a town that had shunned him in the past? What were the chances he would treat the VerHollans with a magnanimity that they had denied him?

What would keep him from taking the girls and moving as far away as he could?

Annie shrugged off the thought. The idea of him taking them away was as absurd as it was frightening. It had taken him two years to come for a week-long visit. The girls would be adults before he would even realize it. He would stay on in Africa and maybe visit occasionally, but Annie really couldn't believe he meant to settle in the States. He was used to Africa and its life-style. Coming back here would be as alien to him as living in Africa would be for Kendall and Jessica. She held tight to the belief that it just couldn't happen—and felt guilty for hoping she was right.

"Do we have to take a nap, Annie? We only take naps in summer. I'm really not tired. Couldn't we just sit on the floor and watch TV? Maybe cartoons are on, or maybe there's a kids' movie on the cable channel or—"

"Kendall, you know that without a nap you won't have any fun tonight. And you know your Uncle Davis will have something special planned. Why don't you both go put on your warm-up suits and then I'll come read you a chapter from *The Little Princess*." It was a bribe, Annie admitted, but a harmless one. The girls seemed placated and she slipped into her room to change out of the sweater dress she'd worn all day.

Finding some slacks that had shed most of their wrinkles, she slipped the wool over her hips and pulled on an angora sweater that was an early Christmas gift from Mary Jane. The warm pastel pink complemented her skin tone and heightened the natural color in her cheeks. She smoothed her clothes and ran a brush through her hair, her thoughts randomly assessing the girls' morning.

The twins had been full of their success. Their father's extravagant praise of their skating prowess only fueled the excitement that came from a morning of exercise and intense concentration. By the time they'd finished a room-service lunch, it was clear to Annie that naps were a necessity.

Pulling her hair into a clip at the back of her head, she tossed the brush into a drawer and left the room. She heard Daniel's voice as she approached the girls' room. The twins were sharing one double bed and Daniel sat in a chair pulled close to the side. He was telling them about African Christmas traditions and they were hanging on every word.

Annie leaned against the doorframe and watched them. Her earlier melancholy had evaporated and she watched the threesome, remaining apart from the group, but included in the aura of the family unit.

Jessica was fighting hard to stay awake, her eyelids fluttering shut now and again. Kendall had her eyes wide open, but Annie recognized the slightly glazed look of fatigue. She turned her attention to Daniel, wondering if he realized how tired they were. In this light Annie could see strands of red and gold in his brown hair. He wore it short, but despite his efforts to control it, the top curled slightly. Annie wondered who cut it for him in Africa. Was there anyone as conventional as a barber on the site or did he have a woman friend who performed the service?

She banished the thought and watched as he encouraged Jessica's comments. His face seemed less harsh, the planes and angles softened by a look that reached his eyes and conveyed his pride and love. Daniel reached over and took Kendall's hand while still listening to Jessica who was more awake now and unusually chatty. The gesture included Kendall in the conversation without letting her dominate. How could he know instinctively how hard it was for Kendall to let anyone else be on center stage? Whatever his reasons, he hadn't stayed away for all those years because he was uncaring. How could anyone who smiled at a child like that be called uncaring?

Tiptoeing away from the room, Annie made herself a cup of tea. Coffee was a stimulant, but for Annie tea was part of the thought process, preparation being a large part of the ritual. At home she would stand at the counter and measure loose leaves into the teapot that had been her grandmother's and wait patiently for the water to boil. Here there were only teabags and a microwave, but Annie decided she would just make do. With a mug of hot tea, she sat in one of the wing-backed chairs by the fireplace. Sipping carefully, she listened for the soft rumble of Daniel's voice as he finished his story. Subconsciously identifying the other sounds of the hotel suite, Annie sorted through the part she had played in the estrangement of Daniel and his children.

The drink helped clear her perspective. She recalled the year after Kathy died. No one ever suggested that Daniel come for the holidays. In her monthly letter she'd invited him for Thanksgiving. It had been a perfunctory suggestion. After all, years had passed and he'd never come before. He hadn't responded to her invitation until a week after the holiday, claiming that the letter had arrived too late for him to make plans. After hearing his story about the political instability in the region, she was more willing now to believe that the mail had been delayed.

Two years ago, she'd harrumphed over the weak excuse. After that she'd tried once more at Christmas, not sure whether his previous explanation had just been a convenient out or the truth. When he never even responded to that invitation, she'd given up the effort. Now she wondered if he'd ever gotten the letter at all. Would he have come if she'd insisted his presence would be welcome?

For the first time Annie wondered if Kathy had ever invited him. When was the last time Kathy had tried to get him to come home and be with his children? Now he was home and Kathy was gone. It was really such a shame. Celebrating Christmas was something that should be shared by people who loved each other, not by a couple whose only bond was two children. But then maybe that was precisely why Daniel hadn't come before. Kendall and Jessica would have been their only bond. The love that Daniel and Kathy had once shared had been long gone, divorce the official acknowledgment of that. Maybe Daniel had wanted to spare the girls the tension that Annie felt now.

At least the three Marshalls were enjoying themselves. Daniel was so natural with the twins. How odd when he'd spent so little time around children. She considered the notion that perhaps he had a family in Africa. She envisioned a bunch of barefoot, dark-haired little boys running around in shorts and T-shirts. But that was her imagination running overtime. If he were married, surely he would have mentioned his wife. Besides, if he had remarried he would be in Africa with that family, not here with them. No, there was no other family, just this broken one.

She jumped up from the chair, disgusted with herself for her wild imaginings. That was what came from a fitful night's sleep and too much free time, she decided. At home she would be in the middle of baking and attending a dozen parties given by every group in town. There would have been the mayor's Open House and the Christmas Charity Walk through the finest homes all decorated for the season. The last sip of her tea acted like a truth serum. Annie admitted she didn't miss any of it, but she did miss being busy.

Her mental list of "things to do" was short, but there were a few items that needed her attention, like the giant stack of gifts crammed into two suitcases hidden in the back of her closet. She'd had a hard time explaining the extra bags to the girls, but they had accepted her second or third attempt.

They probably have it all figured out, she decided, as she pulled the first bag from the back of the closet. She tugged and pulled and tried to remember when she first began to suspect Santa Claus looked remarkably like her Uncle Andrew. How much longer would the twins believe that Santa left them the gifts so carefully arranged under the tree?

She'd spread the contents of the first bag on the bed, when there was a light tap on the door. Visions of a premature end to the Santa tradition sent Annie to the door with unaccustomed speed.

Opening the door slowly, she peered out through the crack. Daniel stood there, shaking his head and smiling at her. Once again she was sure the smile was laughter trying desperately to escape. Yes, he was definitely laughing at her.

"Annie, there's no doubt you move quietly enough to be a great thief, but that open face of yours would give everything away. I suppose you're wrapping presents in there." She nodded. "Want some help?"

She wasn't sure she did, but couldn't think of a gracious way to refuse him. After all, he'd paid for most of them. "Sure." She shrugged. Annie stepped back into the room and moved presents and wrapping material to the floor. Somehow the two of them sitting on her bed, even if it was just to wrap presents, was too intimate to contemplate. Better to be on the floor, preferably with most of the room between them.

She piled the presents between them with the wrappings to the side. She handed Daniel the extra set of scissors and tape she'd brought for the girls to use. He leaned back against a chair and watched her organize the supplies.

"This is some operation. Tell me, do the VerHollans still reuse paper from year to year?"

Annie gestured toward a stack of carefully folded paper. "We surely do. No one can accuse my mother of forgetting the economy of the war years."

"Oh, no. Do they still go on about that?"

Annie wanted to defend her parents, but couldn't deny the truth. "On and on. You'd think the war ended yesterday."

Daniel fingered the paper and checked the size of a piece covered with angels. "Well, this is one tradition I kind of like." Annie watched him and wondered how many other little parts of his life in Georgia were treasured. The sad memories had to far outweigh the good. She was glad he sat here now, sharing one of his happier ones.

He pulled a box from the pile. "Do we get to play with the toys before we wrap them?" He poked at the cellophane cover. "Is this a Barbie doll?"

Annie nodded, waiting for some criticism.

He looked at the doll again and then back at Annie. "Looks just like you." He looked at the doll one more time. "Well, with one little exception."

"I know," she responded, straight-faced. "My feet are bigger."

Daniel laughed with her and waved an arm at the pile of presents before him. "How do they keep from being the most spoiled kids in America?"

Annie wanted to take offense, but couldn't. "I worry about that, too. For the last two years I've made them pick out a charity to contribute something to. Then they do little jobs for me and earn money to send to that charity. When they get a little older, I'd like to get them more personally involved, but..." Her voice trailed off as she realized that the twins might not be a part of her future.

If Daniel was aware of her concern, he didn't let on. "Good idea." He spoke with a mouthful of candy Annie had originally intended as stocking stuffers.

The two began to cut, wrap and beribbon the packages. It didn't take long for Annie to realize that Daniel was hardly a pro at wrapping. He struggled with a simple square box unable to angle the corners with any precision at all.

She sat back and watched him a moment until he looked her way. "Haven't had much practice at this, hmm?"

"Jeez, this is worse than rigging a temporary well in the desert." He dropped the paper and box in disgust. "Maybe I'll just watch you."

"No, you will not." She moved across the floor, closer to where he was sitting. Smoothing the mangled piece of paper, Annie grabbed a box and put on her best "teacher's" voice. "Now Daniel, you're an engineer. This should be a piece of cake for you."

Sitting beside him, she wrapped the paper around the package and taped it together, then turned to look at him.

"Annie, that part I can do. Keep going."

She began to turn the corners into the familiar triangle shape. He watched the first time and nodded slowly. When she started the second side, he reached out and stilled her hand.

"Wait. Go slower," he begged.

She jerked her hand away from his touch, then turned red at her reaction. She tried to concentrate on the package in front of her and ignore the shock of awareness that flashed through her. But now she'd lost her dexterity and had to refold the corner twice before she was satisfied. She wasn't surprised when Daniel commented on it.

"It's good to know even you pro package wrappers occasionally have a little trouble." He reached around her and picked up a game in a small rectangular box. "I'll try this one."

His arm brushed along her leg and Annie shot him a quick look wondering if he was deliberately teasing her. Or was he as surprised as she was at the flash of awareness a moment ago? He appeared engrossed in the description of the game and only glanced up when she moved back over to her side of the room, a much safer three feet away.

He seemed oblivious to the havoc he had caused. "Isn't this game a little advanced for them?"

Annie shook her head. "Maybe, but I do think they're ready to move beyond Candyland."

It took twice as long as it would have if she'd been working alone. Daniel had to look at, examine, and comment on each present he wrapped. And every once in a while she found that she was just sitting there talking to him, mostly about her shopping expeditions and the girls' Christmas lists.

As they worked and chatted, Annie watched Daniel. He became more adept at the wrapping process, but was still cautious in his selections, choosing only the regular shapes, leaving the soccer ball and miniature hot-air balloon for her.

They were down to the last two when Daniel picked up a flat package with no identifying mark on it.

"What's this one?" He shook it a little and was about to open it, when Annie flew across the space between them and tried to grab the box.

"Don't open that!" She made a swipe for it, but Daniel held onto his end, forcing her closer until he fell back and Annie tumbled on top of him. With a deft movement, he rolled her to her back and held her there with one hand on her shoulder as he pulled the package out of her hand.

She was breathless, but not from the exertion. "That's one of your presents." She stared up at him, trying to ignore the way their legs were entwined, the way his hand felt on her shoulder, reminding herself how much she disliked this man. Her brain was short-circuiting though, and all she could feel was a sharp awareness that made speech impossible.

For a moment Daniel looked as though he wouldn't release her. They were so close she could see the dark ring around his iris and the little grey flecks that added warmth to the blue. Then she felt his mood change. His eyes lost their warmth and he carefully removed his hand. Sitting up straight, he offered her a hand, pulling her into an upright position.

Handing her the package, he picked up the last one, a teddy bear that would be hell to wrap. "That one's mine, huh?" He looked at the pile of wrapped packages beside him. "One out of twenty-five. That's not bad."

Despite the tumultuous state of her emotions, Annie laughed at his casual sarcasm. "It's not the quantity, it's the quality that counts."

"What's that?" he asked. "Line twelve from the parents' stock phrase handbook?"

"No," she answered, "line twelve is *It's better to give than to receive*."

He laughed and the intensity of the moment vanished and with it some of the tension that had surrounded them since their arrival. The shared chore had alleviated the ill will. The playful squabble over the present had Annie, at least, questioning some of her actions. If she'd never acknowledged the elemental attraction she'd felt around Daniel, what else had she ignored? What other judgments were suspect? It almost didn't matter. For now she took joy from the fact that they'd spent better than an hour together without a cross word.

With the last of the presents wrapped, they agreed to hide them in the closet in Daniel's room. Annie ran to check on the girls, then helped Daniel with the last two trips.

With the presents safely hidden, Annie busied herself tidying up her room. She hoped keeping her hands busy would keep her from dwelling on more troublesome thoughts, like how charming Daniel was, how irresistible he could be, and the way she'd felt for those few moments when she thought he was going to kiss her.

Chapter Five

This doesn't look much like a residential neighborhood, does it?" Annie whispered the words and Daniel wanted to reassure her. Unfortunately, he shared the same doubt.

The girls sat nestled on either side of them staring earnestly out the windows though there wasn't much to see. Fog added a dense mist to the air. The moisture coated the old cobbled street and the cab slid to the curb and bounced gently against the raised cement edging.

"Are you sure this is the address I gave you?" Daniel spoke to the cabbie while looking out the window in an attempt to spot a street number on the unlit buildings. He wasn't about to abandon the taxi before he was sure they were at the right address. The driver might be surly, but the cab did offer some measure of protection to Annie and the girls.

"Right street? Hey, I been driving a cab twenty years. I know the city. This is it."

It wouldn't be the first time Davis had given him the wrong address. There was an avenue in Paris he knew intimately, all because Davis had inverted the numbers. On the other hand, this neighborhood *was* typical Davis. He probably did live here. It would be just like him to redo the exterior in "early American warehouse."

"So, you want to get out or just think about it? The meter's running."

Annie leaned forward and spoke through the plastic partition that separated passenger from driver. "Do you suppose you could wait a moment while we check and see if this is the right place? Surely you don't want the children to wait in the cold?"

The cabbie's response was grudging but civil: "Gotta keep the meter running."

Daniel was out of the cab before he finished the sentence.

The street was well lit despite the disreputable-looking buildings. He found number thirty-two and approached an imposing steel door to discover a discreetly placed intercom. He pushed the button for the unit marked three and waited, glancing around. The street wasn't so intimidating now, just different from the usual New York address.

He looked back toward the cab and gave them a reassuring wave. Annie smiled back and raised her hand in salute.

Daniel turned back toward the door with a jerk. *That smile.* He'd come armed with enough resentment to resist any overture, but that smile was like a potent drug. He'd done his best to resist its temptation. But ever since their afternoon gift-wrapping session he had to admit it was a losing battle.

The last of his defenses had been sabotaged completely in those few moments he'd held Annie in his arms. However innocent the teasing, there had been nothing innocent in the way his imagination had responded to the intimacy of her body against his. He'd wanted to kiss her. In all honesty, the startled look in her eyes was the only thing that had kept him from pressing his mouth to hers.

If the poinsettia hadn't arrived, he would probably still be regretting the missed opportunity. But the plant and the accompanying note from Roy reminded him that he was probably just one on a long list who found her smile irresistible.

He tried to resurrect those years-old feelings of ill will and resentment, reminding himself that she probably had a list of conquests that covered three counties. But try as he might, he'd lost the armor of ill feeling. It had been thoroughly undermined by the time they'd spent together—talking, sharing experiences. Annie listened, really listened, and she learned from those insights, Daniel was sure of it.

Still he couldn't resist a healthy dose of skepticism. How could a few heartfelt conversations bridge years of animosity? It was just too good to be true. It was also a sure sign that he'd lost all his good sense if he let himself be taken in by a sweet smile.

But her smile was more than sweet. It was a smile enticingly packaged in a body that teased his senses with every move. And that only made it worse—clouding the issue, making it more difficult to understand his motives.

He punched the button again as if he were summoning an antidote to the attraction he felt.

The door creaked open and Davis Marshall grabbed his brother in a bear hug. "How you doin', bro? Is it good to see you! It's been too long, much too long."

Daniel nodded and returned the embrace.

The cabdriver leaned on the horn and both men headed for the corner. Davis opened the passenger door and called back to Daniel, "You pay the man while I say hello to this woman you're no longer related to."

Daniel paid the driver and turned to watch the mutual admiration society that spilled onto the sidewalk. The girls were jumping up and down while Davis hugged Annie.

There was a time he and Davis could have passed for twins, but his brother had stopped growing a few inches sooner; his hair was just a bit curlier and considerably longer than Daniel's conservative cut. He looked good, Daniel thought. His gypsy life-style seemed to agree with him.

They hurried into the lobby of the building and onto a large freight elevator. All the while, Davis kept up inconsequential chatter. "Been to see Santa? How about Rockefeller Center? What did you think of FAO Schwartz?"

When Kendall asked, "Who's he?" Davis feigned shock.

"Not a person, sweetie, just the greatest toy store in the world. And you haven't been there yet? We'll have to take care of that."

The elevator came to a smooth stop on the third floor and they were in a long narrow hall with one door. Davis opened it and stepped back.

Daniel's first thought was that Davis did live in a warehouse. His second was that he'd decorated the place for Christmas. Then he realized the neon signs and carousel animals were part of the usual decor. The entry space was cut off from the rest of the loft by an eight-foot wall. On it hung a flashing neon sign that read The Chat and Chew. Lined along the wall were pegs, full of coats, as though the loft was home to more than one man. Davis doubled up a few of the coats and made space for his guests' things. The girls followed Davis into the living area, Kendall forging ahead, Jessica timidly following her sister's lead.

"Good heavens, this is incredible!" Annie was next to Daniel, her words a whisper.

He turned toward her and nodded. "It certainly is, but it's typical. Life's a party to Davis. His motto is Get the Job Done and Get On with the Fun."

"It's like a giant playpen." Annie stood still in the doorway, while Davis showed the girls around.

Daniel took Annie's arm. "Come on in. He wants everyone to have as much fun as he does."

For the first hour Davis played with the girls, including Annie, letting the twins climb on the wooden carousel animals and explaining some of the more unconventional items. He had a sentimental attachment to some of them, but others were rejects he'd rescued from the toy designer who lived downstairs.

"Daddy, daddy, look at this!" Jessica came running over, sliding on the polished wood floor, grabbing her father's hand. "This is our favorite."

It was a mechanized aquarium, complete with plastic fish that responded to some subtle current in the water. The fish swam erratically around the water-filled tank and the girls insisted they were real. Davis let himself be convinced and asked the girls to name them.

Davis forgot dinner. Annie offered to stop at the nearest grocery and pick up chicken or steaks.

"Not necessary, Annie. Chinese takeout was made for occasions like this."

Daniel strongly suspected his children had never tasted Chinese food before. It wasn't the sort of cuisine that was popular in Avon. But the chopsticks Davis produced made eating a game and the girls never thought to question the shrimp balls, fried rice and moo goo gai pan.

"I think the only reason you want us to use these things is so you can get more to eat." Annie dropped the chopsticks and grabbed Davis by the arm. Her voice was theatrical, her gestures pure Sarah Bernhardt. "We're dying of hunger. Where are the forks?"

Clustered around the low table and cushions that served as the dining space, the five of them made a party out of the meal. Davis seemed to bring out the craziness in everyone. Annie teased Davis about his chopstick expertise and then mimicked a redneck's disdain for "foreign food." She was always upbeat and smiling, but Daniel had never realized she could be downright funny.

She sat, entranced, as Davis told one story after another about the year he'd spent in Hong Kong working on a series of films for British television.

Daniel wondered if her fascination was just an act. She'd listened to stories of his childhood with the same single-minded attention. Was it just an ego-stroking exercise? Did she listen to her neighbor discuss the church service with as much interest? Probably. He wondered if it came naturally, or if she'd rehearsed that attentive expression.

Everyone shifted the plates and half-finished cartons to the kitchen. While Annie washed the few dishes, Davis stashed the leftovers in a refrigerator crammed with similar boxes. Daniel kept an eye on Kendall and Jessica, who wandered around the cluttered open space playing with whatever toy caught their eye.

Daniel leaned against the kitchen counter and wished for his pipe. He could tell Annie's fascination wasn't one-sided. Davis, too, seemed caught in the web of Annie's charm, coming up with one outrageous story after another just to make her laugh or shake her head in disbelief. Who would have thought one charmer would be so susceptible to another? He'd always thought it was the introspective, intense types like himself who found an infectious smile so irresistible.

And she *was* irresistible. Her spontaneity and warmth were like a magnet to someone like him. She'd drawn more from him in the last week than he'd shared with anyone in years. Now Davis was hooked, telling stories he'd stockpiled for five years. Daniel felt like a teenager who's just discovered that his girl is about to date his buddy. He wanted to punch Davis and drag Annie home where she would save her smiles just for him.

Did she have this effect on every man?

He hadn't considered picking a fight with his brother in ten years. It was bad enough he was thinking like a teenager, there was no reason to act like one. Daniel eased himself from the adult group and went to find his children. He followed the sounds of electronic beep and squeak and tracked them down in front of some Oriental video game that was proving difficult to master.

"Daddy!" They dropped the joysticks as soon as they saw him. "Daddy, will you show us how to play this game over here?"

Pulling him toward the window, they pointed to a classic pinball machine. Daniel smiled. He recognized the machine. He and Davis had spent hours trying to best one like it when they'd spent three days waiting out bad weather in Greenland. They'd been returning to the States for their first experience at boarding school.

He pulled a chair over so the girls could see the flashing, whirling gates and slides of the "Universe at War." He gathered a handful of quarters from his pocket, had Jessica slip one in the slot and pulled back the plunger to release the first ball. A welter of memories coursed through him. Distracted as he was by the flood of feeling, the first ball made its way through the course with no lights or bells.

Kendall was disappointed. "Is that all?"

Daniel shook off his reverie with a laugh at his daughter. "I'm out of practice, honey. Let's try it again." He stepped aside. "Here, you pull the knob back and let it go and I'll show you how to rack up the points."

With the girls watching, he did justice to the next ball and soon he could feel his old form returning. He shared flippers with his fan club and soon they were engrossed in the numbers flashing past on the scoreboard.

When the twins won their first free game they were hooked, and Daniel stepped back to let them try their own luck.

The teamwork lasted exactly five minutes. Then Kendall insisted that she have a chance "to do it alone."

Jessica tolerated that for exactly one ball. "My turn!" she shouted.

Kendall said no. Jessica insisted. Kendall ignored her. Jessica reached over and sabotaged the game. Kendall pushed her sister off the chair and Jessica ran crying to her father.

Daniel watched the scenario unfold and felt powerless to stop it. He was annoyed at the girls for spoiling the game, but more embarrassed because he didn't know how to handle the situation. Should he berate the teary Jessica for not being patient, or should he punish Kendall for pushing her sister off the chair? He stood, absently patting Jessica on the head, trying to decide.

"I think it's time to go home," Annie's breath was soft on his ear as she whispered her suggestion. He turned and looked at her, their faces inches apart.

She smiled an apology as though she were responsible for their behavior. "This is the way they behave when they're overexcited. How about if you give Jessie a cuddle and I'll try to pry Kendall away from the pinball machine?"

Daniel nodded and scooped Jessica into his arms. He stood a moment and watched as Annie began a one-sided conversation with Kendall. It wasn't hard to figure out that Kendall wasn't in the mood to cooperate. In the end Annie scooped up the remaining quarters and walked toward the door. Kendall stood stubbornly by the machine, as if willing it to start up without its offering. When it didn't, she turned around and screamed, "I don't wanna go back to the hotel!"

The next two hours were not pleasant. Daniel was sure he was seeing his children at their worst. At least he *hoped* this was their worst. He was able to hold on to his patience by letting Annie cope with the bickering and tearful pleading. He followed her directions and supervised the toothbrush detail. Then he watched while she tried to settle the girls down. She finally separated them, putting Jessica in Daniel's bedroom so she wouldn't have to bear the brunt of Kendall's displeasure. There were no stories that night, no late-night giggle sessions. Daniel felt nothing but admiration for Annie when the twins were in darkened rooms and the adults could settle close by the fire for a nightcap.

He sat down with a huge sigh of relief.

Annie took a sip of the white wine Daniel had poured for her. "I'm not even sure I said good-night to Davis."

"Sure you did. Right after Jessica pinched Kendall's arm and before Kendall countered with that dandy hair-pull."

She held up her hand. "Please! Spare me the details. What a nightmare! Do you think we should let them go with Davis tomorrow? He doesn't have much experience with kids."

"Yeah, he's not much more than an overgrown kid himself. But don't you think we've earned a break? Especially you. I can see I've got a lot to learn about parenting."

They sat inches apart on one of the love seats, Annie absently watching the flames in the fireplace, Daniel watching Annie. She pushed a stray strand of hair behind her ear and took another sip of wine. "When it comes to parenting, I don't know how much is learned and how much is the will to survive. When they're like that, I forget everything I've ever read and just operate on instinct. Thank God it doesn't happen very often."

Annie paused a moment. "If I really were an expert, I would have seen it coming. They reach a point where they're overtired and overexcited, and then I've got my hands full."

Daniel stretched an arm along the back of the seat and put his feet up on the low table. "I never behaved that way when I was tired. I just found a corner and went to sleep. They must have inherited that from your side of the family."

She rolled her eyes and shook her head. "It won't wash, Daniel. Davis told me that you were a master at the punch-and-run."

Daniel straightened in indignation. "Davis said that? Hey, he was always getting me into scrapes I got blamed for because—"

"You were the oldest. He said you'd say that."

Daniel felt, and was sure he looked affronted, but only for a moment. Then he laughed out loud.

Annie put her feet up on the table, too, and sighed. "I had fun with Davis, but I'm glad to be back here. No wonder the girls were so wired. I've never seen so many strange toys in one place. It was wild, wasn't it?"

Daniel nodded. "Like I said, it's Davis to a T."

"I'm sure he's the greatest brother in the world, but not the sort of person you'd turn to for rest and relaxation." She leaned her head back, resting it on his arm. "I don't mean to sound critical, Daniel, but what does he do for common sense? Some of those stories he told . . . I tell you I wonder how he stays alive when he's on those remote shoots."

"When we were growing up, staying alive was always my specialty. I remember once when he wanted to dive into an old quarry and another time when he wanted to try and hand-feed a nursing elephant." Daniel shook his head. "Maybe he's found some other lifeguard."

Annie sat up straight again and turned her full attention to Daniel. "He's fun, but honestly, Daniel, I can only stand so much of that frenetic good humor. Wasn't it hard growing up with him?"

Daniel tried to hide his smile. "Well, I used to sneak out, climb a certain tree and read a lot."

They shared a smile of perfect understanding. That smile erased all the pangs of jealousy that had grown over the past few hours. He actually felt a moment's sympathy for Davis.

He reached over for his glass of wine and caught sight of the red-blooming poinsettia sitting on the hearth. Of course, Roy was still a factor.

He took a sip of the wine and savored the flavor.

Maybe Roy was nothing more than a friend. Would a lover send something as impersonal as a poinsettia? If it had been him, Daniel decided, he would have sent white roses or maybe even red ones.

"What do you suppose this green thing is?" Daniel pointed to a carefully colored blob at the foot of the Christmas tree Jessica had drawn just before her nap. Today was the day they were going to FAO Schwartz with Davis. The tantrums of the night before were still fresh in their memory. Hoping to avoid a similar episode, both adults had insisted the girls take a nap.

Annie looked up from the button she was tightening on Kendall's coat. "The green thing? It's a cat curled up waiting for Santa."

"That's amazing." He squinted at it, trying to bring the image of a cat into focus. Was it possible his daughter had eye problems? "Are you sure?"

She nodded.

"How do you know?"

Annie looked at Daniel. "I'd love to have you think I'm some kind of omniscient Earth Mother, but that wouldn't be fair." She shrugged. "I asked her what it was."

"I suppose that's a technique you learned from your mother?"

Annie shook her head. "No, Mary Jane. She teaches first grade, remember? According to her, you never make an aesthetic judgment of your own without knowing what you're critiquing. You might say something like 'Oh, what a lovely washing machine,' and the little ego will be crushed because what they really drew was a cow."

"How could you mix up a cow with a washing machine?"

She laughed. "How could you mix up a cat and green blob?"

Daniel nodded slowly, then leaned close across the back of the couch. "Do you remember the first picture that Jessica sent me after I went back to Africa?"

"The purple giraffe?"

"Is that what it was? I was so thrilled to get something from her I framed it and put it on my dresser. But all this time I thought it was a purple high-rise building. I always wondered why she'd send me a picture of a high rise, but it was a giraffe, huh? Now that makes a lot more sense."

He came close and sat on the chair across from her. He leaned toward her, clasping his hands together and waited a moment until he had her full attention.

"I can't tell you how much their pictures and your letters meant to me. It was the first time in years that someone was interested in something besides the check I sent every month. I remember thinking that you and your mother were a lot alike."

Annie stopped her mending and looked up. It wasn't often she didn't smile. She wasn't now. Daniel sat back in his chair wondering what he could possibly have said to wipe the smile off her face.

"Exactly how does writing you a letter make me like my mother?"

The question, or maybe her tone, told him volumes about her relationship with Lillian VerHollan. He couldn't resist smiling at her sulky expression. It was endearing and very sexy.

"Maybe I used the wrong word there. I was thinking about her mania for staying in touch. Maybe you're not so much *like* your mother as you are *inspired* by her?" He felt like some State Department spokesman, trying to work his way out of a misspoken phrase.

She seemed slightly mollified. "There's a big difference between asking you to write to your children occasionally and my mother's 'mania.'"

He nodded, considering the comparison. "You're right. There was nothing the slightest bit annoying about those letters and pictures the girls sent." He didn't have to say how annoying Lillian's constant phone calls could be. He could see it was one of the things they agreed upon.

Annie resumed the mending. "Besides, I didn't do that for myself. I did it so the girls would know they had a father. I told you once before they're reaching an age when Daddy is important to them."

"Well, whatever your motivation, I thank you."

Annie shrugged and finished her mending. He watched her face as she worked. She smiled at her handiwork, made a grimace when she missed the correct hole in the button, frowned at the knot. Even in repose her face was animated. She bit off the thread and set the work aside.

She sat back, her expression questioning. "I've always wondered about something, Daniel."

"What something is that?" He did have a hard time following her thought patterns. What was she wondering about? Why buttons fall off new coats? Why he liked to sit and watch her? Why he had a hard time thinking about anything but her smile?

"Why you never wrote to the girls after you went to Africa."

Would she ever stop reviewing each past mistake? When would she stop analyzing him and just accept him for the man he was? It wasn't as though his bad choices had affected the balance of power or destroyed the country's economic base.

He sat weighing his thoughts a moment. In all honesty his mistakes had been worse. He knew Annie believed that, and he could see the truth in it himself. His mistakes couldn't affect the national debt, but they had influenced his children's lives. He'd hurt Kendall and Jessica. As much as he wanted to make amends now, he would have to deal with past mistakes before he could go on. Maybe all Annie's questions were her way of trying to find some ground for forgiveness. At least he hoped they were.

"In fact, I did write at first. But the girls were so young. And then Kathy never answered any of my letters, never sent pictures. After a while I just gave up."

He didn't want to sound maudlin, so he stopped there. He didn't tell her about watching toddlers in the villages and wondering about the twins. Every time he was in the capital and saw European and American kids, he would wonder if they were learning the same things as his own.

"It really was a one-sided effort?"

"All I can say is, I must have written twenty times asking her to write or send some pictures."

"And she never did?"

"Once or twice she sent pictures." And he'd treasured them, worn them ragged from handling. "But they were always pictures with your parents. I was sure they were designed to show me exactly how well they were doing without me."

"And you believed that, Daniel?"

Her disappointment needled him. Yes, he'd done exactly as Kathy had hoped. He'd given up, let her win the war of attrition. Now Annie was blaming him for that, for not fighting harder. He stood up and walked behind the love seat. "I decided that maybe they were better off without me. The thing is, they were so small. They needed their mother. So finally I stopped trying and just sent the checks."

He watched her as a shadow of regret replaced the disappointment. "It must have been so hard for you."

Her sympathy was a total surprise. He nodded and her understanding drew the words from his heart. "I was lonely, more lonely than I've ever been in my life. I guess I could have tried harder. But I buried myself in my work and tried to forget the pain."

He tried to come up with some rationalization. "It was so long ago, before Kathy died, and I realized how important those kids were to me. It was before I saw them again, before you insisted they become a part of my life."

"You were the only parent they had left." Annie spoke with urgency as though she were trying to convince him, or maybe herself, that she'd done the right thing. "When you came for the funeral they treated you like a stranger. That just wasn't right. I thought that if they wrote to you, when you came to see them again, they might feel more comfortable around you." *Have I made a terrible mistake?* Her expression was as eloquent as the unspoken words.

How could she come this far, then doubt the wisdom of her actions? Maybe because she was beginning to accept the fact that he wasn't the villain the rest of her family had painted. At the thought a flurry of joy, of pure happiness settled in his heart. "Well, it worked, didn't it? They don't seem the slightest bit inhibited." Did she need any more proof than that?

They both smiled. "Honestly, Daniel, how could they feel inhibited around a man who sends them the world's worst knock-knock jokes?"

Chapter Six

A sleepy-eyed Kendall interrupted. Jessica followed close behind. Nap time was over and so was any more meaningful conversation. The girls were looking forward to their outing with Davis, who was due in less than an hour.

While she poured the last of the milk and Daniel opened a package of cookies, Annie voiced her worries about letting Davis take the children for the afternoon.

Daniel thumped the cookie package on the counter and turned toward her. "You be careful, young lady, or I'm going to be tempted to compare you to your mother again."

Annie didn't know whether to laugh or be offended. He was teasing, but the underlying truth took most of the humor out of the comment.

"It really will be okay, Annie. Davis can be a responsible adult when the situation calls for it."

Annie put the milk on a tray and Daniel added the plateful of cookies. "I'm not that concerned about their safety, Daniel. I'm just a little worried about exactly what they'll bring back from the toy store."

"I know what you mean. The same thing's occurred to me. But since he was due here ten minutes ago, I guess it's a little late to act on our second thoughts."

She really didn't want to cancel the outing. Davis was the twins' uncle, after all. He was entitled to spend some time with them. If the worst thing that came out of it was a life-size stuffed giraffe, what was the problem with that?

This whole vacation was what memories were made of. Once it was over and Daniel was back in Africa, or on to his next project, Kendall and Jessica would have a mere ten days to treasure. And Annie wasn't sure it was the adventures with Davis they would remember best. Bedtime stories with their father, sharing prayers and the hundred other intimacies of daily life—those were the moments that would fuel the love growing between father and daughters.

Moments like the ones she'd observed that morning at the Central Park rink. This time she'd been invited. She'd been there when Daniel urged Jessica to buy the tickets, held her hand to give her courage. She saw his proud smile when Kendall laced her own skates. They'd all laughed when Daniel put his skates on the wrong feet and his daughters helped him relace them. Had he done it on purpose?

She had a few memories of her own. The way he looked walking with a daughter on each arm. The first loop the girls made without falling. The way that Kendall and Jessica discussed their new skating skills when they'd stopped for hot chocolate at the little coffee shop near the hotel.

The twins were standing at the window now, five floors up, hoping to see Davis arriving. She prayed the nap would see them through the rest of the day in good humor. An instant replay of last night's temper tantrum was definitely not a memory she would cherish.

Kendall abandoned her stance by the window and began hovering near the door, so when Davis announced his arrival with a rhythmic knock, she flung the door open enthusiastically.

Davis exploded into the room, inspected the space, kissed Annie, shook Daniel's hand and announced he had a car waiting. The girls scrambled into coats and boots, found gloves and ran for the elevator in less than five minutes.

Daniel looked as dazed as Annie felt. Davis was almost out the door when he leaned back around the panel. "You two have a reservation for tea at the Pierre at four. Don't be late. You wouldn't want to get on any maître d's blacklist."

Annie stood staring at the door. Tea? He'd made a reservation for tea? How perfectly civilized. Was it his way of guaranteeing that she and Daniel would be polite to each other for the few hours he was gone? If they were in a public space they could hardly cause a scene.

Maybe Davis didn't realize that any inclination she'd had to argue had died long ago. On the other hand, she wasn't sure that their truce was ready for expansion.

Tea at the Pierre did sound charming, sophisticated, intimate. Maybe too intimate. Wouldn't it be easier to preserve the peace if the two of them just went their separate ways? Daniel could read a book; she could do a little totally unnecessary shopping. They could sort of peacefully coexist. The whole object of this vacation was to bring Daniel closer to his children. No one said the adults had to be budding, as well.

On the other hand, no one ever had tea in Avon—at least not tea as a meal. Surely it would be foolish to pass up such a splendid experience just because she was afraid of a little conversation.

"I take it a tea party doesn't appeal to you?"

Daniel's flat question recalled her from her speculation and she looked up. He was standing behind the counter of the wet bar and she had his full attention.

He was bristling again, expecting her to reject the idea out of hand. Despite the fact that was exactly what she was tempted to do, she shook her head. "Why no, it sounds wonderful. I was just thinking it would be a very civilized way to spend the afternoon."

"The truth is, my little brother likes to meddle."

Annie smiled at his calculated tone, suddenly determined to talk him into an outing she had had doubts about until five seconds ago.

"So, how bad can it be, hmm? Tea and crumpets and we'll watch all the sweet little old ladies who make it a ritual." She couldn't believe that she was talking him into it. For just a moment she wondered if he really wanted to go, but didn't want to be the one to say so. "Oh, come on, Daniel, you know it'll be fun, an experience, maybe even an adventure."

"I'll settle for an experience, an adventure I can do without. Tell me, what does one wear to tea?"

They discussed clothes for a moment and retired to their rooms to dress. He'd been awfully easy to convince. Hopefully, he had a list of neutral things to talk about. She was completely out of meaningless conversations.

Annie pulled out the sweater dress she'd already worn and changed the look with an oversize silk scarf. She combed her hair and added a little color to her eyes and mouth. Her cheeks rarely needed blush and today they seemed more pink than usual, probably from the nippy winter air.

All the while she tried to think of suitable teatime conversation. They could always talk about the girls' academic achievements. But numbers and a grade-one primer wouldn't take them too far.

She dug out her good purse and gloves and spent two minutes trying to remember where she'd put her angora beret.

Good heavens, they couldn't talk about her family without fighting, the latest goings-on in Avon wouldn't interest him in the slightest. And she hadn't gotten around to reading the paper since she'd left home. What *would* they talk about?

She found the light blue scrap of a hat and went into the living area. Daniel was waiting and exhibiting none of the nervousness she felt.

The Pierre was a short walk away. The fog and damp of the previous day had evaporated and the air was clear and invigorating, like a deep winter day in Georgia.

Nothing else reminded her of home. The streets were crowded. Women in fur coats were common, even a few men wore them. Everyone had armloads of packages. Bell ringers were on almost every street corner collecting donations for various charities. The hand-rung bells and the smell of chestnuts roasting put a touch of Christmas in the air. Annie lost herself in the sensations and welcomed the exhilaration that overwhelmed her. The air was so perfect that she almost suggested hot chocolate in the park, but changed her mind when a random gust of wind turned the bracing air biting.

They slipped through the revolving door into the warmth and tranquillity of the Pierre. Annie looked around, too impressed to try to disguise the fact that she was a tourist. Wouldn't Mary Jane love this! she thought.

The uptown streets hadn't seemed particularly rowdy, but the hotel lobby was so quiet it gave a whole new meaning to the idea of understated elegance. She spared a look at Daniel, who nodded his amazement. He took her arm, leaning close for a moment. "I feel as if we should whisper or we'll be asked to leave." Annie nodded and he added, "Quick, tell me, is my tie too loud?"

Annie laughed warmly and the bellman actually looked their way. Daniel hurried her down the hall that led to the tearoom. The walkway was lined with small boutiques. It was Christmas here, too. Each shop window caught her attention, like so many teasing advertisements. And like the ads in the glossy magazines, Annie admired the jewelry, leather and scarves without ever considering buying one of the pricey items. It was clear Tiffany's didn't have the New York monopoly on luxury items.

A right turn took them into the area that served as the tearoom. There were several other couples waiting to be seated, but when Daniel gave the maître d' his name, they were promptly escorted to a prime spot. The room had the feel of a small but elegant lobby with tables around the periphery. The chairs were upholstered and comfortable. Pure white linens, heavy, well-used silver, formally dressed waiters: tea at the Pierre was definitely an exercise in civility.

The marble floor, elaborate statuary and ornate murals added to the mood of comfort and indulgence. Annie slipped out of her coat, glad they'd decided to dress up a bit.

What else could they order but the traditional English tea? The service was prompt and in a short time they were sampling dainty sandwiches of salmon and cucumber.

Annie sipped her Earl Grey tea and sat back in the chair. "This really is an adult way to play make-believe, isn't it?"

Daniel nodded. "Unless you're English and have enough leisure time to spend an hour sipping, I guess you're right."

"This time of year I'm usually bargaining with God for just a few more hours in the day."

"Lots of parties and Christmas shopping?"

"And baking and school activities. It always takes forever to find the right present for Mother and Daddy." This year she'd commissioned a portrait of the twins. Mary Jane was holding it for her. Hopefully, the picture would mellow her parents' anger at the way she'd—

"What about Roy?"

Daniel's question cut into her musing and she was confused. "What do you mean?"

Daniel leaned forward a little in his chair. "How long does it take you to find him his Christmas present?"

Annie leaned forward, too. "I wish I could disabuse you of the notion that Roy and I are in any way intimate." Good heavens! The tea was even affecting her vocabulary. She sat back in her seat once again and refused to let go of the pleasant atmosphere. "Mary Jane would never forgive me, and besides, he's never been more than a friend."

He looked unconvinced.

"You're wondering about the poinsettia?"

Daniel nodded.

"The girls and I made decorated cookies and a fruitcake for him. That was his thank-you." Where did he ever get the idea that Roy was her beau? The idea was ludicrous. Then again, why was she so anxious to convince Daniel that Roy wasn't anyone "special"? She supposed it was because there were enough misunderstandings between them as it was. This one was easy enough to clear up.

"He's a real tease, Daniel. He's always trying to get a reaction out of Mary Jane. That explains the comment to Jessica about 'marrying a blonde.' He and Mary Jane have been bickering since her black hair was in pigtails. Everyone in town knows it's only a matter of time before the two decide to stop arguing and get married."

"And you'll be maid of honor?"

She smiled. "I might be the best man, too."

"You don't dream about walking down the aisle yourself?"

She was startled by the question. Did she ever dream of getting married? "Not really." She didn't want to say any more on the subject, but Daniel sat quietly, his silence as good as a question. "I suppose it would be wonderful to find someone to share everything with." *Like we've shared the last few days.* "But why build your dreams around some mythical relationship?"

"So what *do* you build your dreams around?"

This wasn't the sort of trivial conversation Annie had had in mind. "Oh, Daniel, you already know all about me. You lived just a few miles away for years."

Daniel nodded in agreement. "Sure I know the basics. But I've told you all about what I hope to do, now I want to know what your plans are. Before Kendall and Jessica were a part of your life, what did you wish for?"

She couldn't imagine why he would want to know about her teenage dreams. She'd almost forgotten them herself. It had been years since those long conversations with Mary Jane. They'd made plans, all right. Staring at her teacup, she spoke out loud, answering his question but not really speaking to him. "I wanted to join the Peace Corps."

Daniel seemed surprised. "You wanted to join the Peace Corps?"

Annie looked at him, annoyed that she'd spoken aloud and even more annoyed at his attitude. Did he find it so difficult to believe that there was a VerHollan with goals beyond what could be found in Avon? She took a sip of her tea and let the warmth soothe her annoyance. She had to agree it wasn't an ambition one normally associated with her family.

"Maybe it was part of the teenage rebellion phase." Then she drew on another fragment of memory. "Actually I think it was Davis's influence. He came to visit right after he signed up, but before he started training."

"I gather nothing came of it."

Annie shook her head reluctantly. "My parents convinced me I could do the same work closer to home."

Daniel nodded in complete understanding. "So Kathy wasn't the only one who got sold the 'family first and always' routine."

If he was trying to make her defensive he was succeeding, but only because he was on target. Her parents had pressured her to stay near home, using every ploy they could think of to make her feel guilty because she was essential to their happiness.

Annie picked up the train of thought. "I didn't buy into the 'family first and always routine' as you call it, at least not completely. I worked for the Head Start Program in Augusta during my college summer vacations. When I graduated they were going to give me a full-time job. I'd even found an apartment in the city. I had plans. Then reality intervened.

"There were budget cutbacks and the job never materialized. Kathy kept asking me to come back to Avon and help with the twins. I found I used all my psychology on those two little tykes. By then those kids were into everything and Kathy really needed help, so I stayed home with her."

Daniel nodded and glanced away. "So, you studied psychology?"

Annie was grateful for the shift in conversation. They were getting too close to sensitive ground when they talked about how much help Kathy needed in those days. "I studied psychology *and* early-childhood education in Augusta."

"Sounds like you were tailor-made for Head Start work."

"During those college years, I wasn't even thinking practical application. For a while, just graduating seemed like a pretty worthwhile goal."

"Too much fun partying?"

"Hardly." Annie shook her head and smiled, recalling how quickly she'd figured out she couldn't major in partying and hope to graduate. "Mind you, I didn't completely abandon the social scene, but it wasn't my major area of study. No, my real nemeses were statistics and biology."

"Those were easy A's for me. Too bad I wasn't around, I could have given you a few pointers."

It was the wrong thing to say, a downright stupid thing to say. Annie remembered her sophomore year very clearly. That had been about the time when Kathy had filed for divorce. At that point, feelings between Daniel and the VerHollans were at an all-time low.

"Well, maybe once I move back to the States, you'll have a chance to resurrect some of those dreams and get on with your life."

"The girls and my parents are my life now, Daniel. Living in Avon may not have been my first choice, but things have changed. My family comes before everything else. I made that choice years ago and now I have to live with it."

"When I come back won't all that change? Or is it more than the girls that keep you there? You've said you're not dreaming of marriage, at least not at the moment. Why do you feel as if you've made some kind of irrevocable choice?"

He looked genuinely puzzled. But that wasn't surprising. Here was a man who'd spent most of his life far from his homeland, moving from mission to mission with only occasional visits to renew those family ties that were the focal point of the VerHollans' life.

"For one thing, I'm not entirely convinced you're coming home as promptly as you insist." She was being generous. She didn't believe for a minute he was about to give up his international life-style. "Beyond that, I've spent all my life in Avon. I have roots there. My family needs me, and not just as a surrogate parent to your daughters."

"I just don't understand why they need you there every minute of every day."

She thought of a hundred ways of responding. It was something he would probably never understand. A way of life so alien to him that trying to explain would only lead to an argument. As it was, they were uncomfortably close to one now and it wasn't the way she wanted to spend the afternoon.

Annie reached across the table and touched his hand. "Daniel, I don't want to have words about this or anything else. This is such a lovely spot. Can't we just put our differences on hold and talk about something neutral?"

He looked as though he was going to press his point, but apparently changed his mind. He squeezed the hand that lay on his. "Sure, but the point is this argument won't go away just because we ignore it."

Annie shrugged her shoulders. "So let's postpone it, and in the meantime, we can pretend we're two people on vacation and loving every minute of it."

Daniel looked away for a moment. "So tell me, what do you think of the weather?"

Annie laughed and then answered. They chatted about the weather and how perfect it was, for New York in December. Still, Daniel found it cold. He admitted that except for one or two skiing holidays, he avoided snow and freezing temperatures, preferring warm, even humid weather.

Annie wondered if he did relocate, would he choose another African post or consider South America? She didn't ask.

The subject of Christmas gifts came up. "Tell the truth, Annie, did you really enjoy shopping for all those presents?"

She smiled. "You sound just like Daddy. His idea of shopping is to settle down with a stack of catalogs, a credit card and the telephone. He's always done by the first week in December."

Daniel nodded. "Sounds good to me."

"I prefer the hands-on approach myself." At Daniel's frown, Annie thought for a moment, searching for the reason why. "I'm afraid that I'll miss the perfect gift. There's always the chance I'll see something I never thought of putting on my list, that little something extra..." She trailed off at his expression. "I'm not convincing you, am I?"

He laughed and shook his head. "I guess what we have here is the classic confrontation of shopper and nonshopper."

"Oh, Daniel, how can you say that when you haven't been in a mall for years?"

"Hey, some of those African markets are a heck of a lot more challenging than any mall on sale day."

Annie agreed. Maybe she was being a little provincial. She tried to imagine Daniel wandering through a bazaar, looking for a new pipe or the dolls for the African village he'd made for the girls. "Is that where you found the dolls for the village?"

He nodded. "As a matter of fact, yes. And I did enjoy that. I'd finished the huts and the animals faster than I thought and considered carving the people, too. But I'm just not that good at detail work.

"I was in the capital for a meeting so I brought it all along to mail and lucked into the dolls at one of the outdoor markets."

That must have been the same week that he'd gotten the notice of the bounced check. She didn't mention it and neither did he.

"Well, it's a wonderful present. I think the rest will pale in comparison."

"I don't know, Annie. That Barbie doll was pretty impressive." Daniel leered suggestively and Annie reached over and slapped his hand playfully. He persisted. "Come on. You mean you've never had one lascivious thought about Ken?"

The idea was so absurd that she laughed out loud.

By the time they left the Pierre, they *were* two people on holiday and truly enjoying it. Annie tucked her hand into the crook of Daniel's arm and the two strolled the few blocks back to their hotel humming Christmas carols and dropping coins into every Salvation Army kettle they passed.

As they crossed the lobby, Annie remembered that she needed to buy some milk for breakfast. Daniel was anxious to check and see if Kendall and Jessica were back, so she encouraged him to go up to their room, while she ducked out for a quart of milk.

On her way back through the lobby the second time, the bellman called Annie's attention to a handful of messages awaiting her. They were all from her mother. Annie had forgotten her promised phone call and Lillian VerHollan was obviously frantic.

With a groan Annie hurried to the elevator, fingering the slips of pink paper, already formulating some soothing phrases she hoped would placate her mother.

Annie fished in her pocket for the room key. As she pushed the door open she could hear Daniel's voice, but no answering sound from the children. They weren't there and Daniel was on the phone.

"I've already explained, Lillian. Annie went to get some milk; the children are out with my brother."

He listened a moment. "Last night we were out quite late and it took the twins a long time to settle down. I'm sure Annie just forgot to call. She was tired, too."

He stood still and controlled, but despite his attempt to sound calm Annie could feel the anger emanating from him, the effort it took to measure his words and be civil.

She threw her coat onto the stool near the bar and motioned for him to give her the phone.

"Just a minute, Lillian, Annie's just walked in." He covered the mouthpiece. "Annie, honey, I'm sorry. She sounds as though she thinks I've murdered all of you and hid the remains."

In explanation, Annie handed him the pink message slips and took the phone. She prayed a moment for divine inspiration and said hello.

Annie recognized her mother's five-minute monologue on thoughtless children. She listened to the first few statements, decided she felt guilty enough and interrupted—or tried to.

"Mother."

"I just don't see how you could forget that call—"

"Mother."

"Your father said the police would call if something awful had happened."

"Mother."

Lillian VerHollan would not be distracted. Annie gave up and listened, or pretended to. She resented the interruption, just when she'd begun to enjoy herself. She was embarrassed that Daniel was a witness to the very thing he resented most about her parents: their possessiveness.

"But so many little things could have happened that the police would never know about. You could have broken your arm, and heaven knows that Daniel would never call—"

"Mother, just listen to me, please. Everything is fine. As Daniel said, it took forever to get the girls to settle down last night and then I just thought it was too late to call." In fact, Daniel had been more honest, she *had* completely forgotten the call. Hopefully, the Lord would forgive her the slight twist.

"Where are the children?"

The conversation went on and on, Annie answering her mother's hundred questions as simply as possible and hoping that the long-distance operator would call time. It was the only way her mother would ever get off the phone.

It was her father who came to the rescue. "Wallace says I have to hang up now. But he says not to forget to call again. Both of us have been sick with worry. It's just been the most awful Christmas. I hope—"

"Mother, things are going very well here. I'm sorry you're not having fun, but it's all in a good cause." Annie hung up the phone, certain her mother would have gone on with her goodbye until Annie felt guilty enough to agree to anything. She tried so hard to do what was right and still keep everyone happy. Why couldn't her mother cooperate just a little?

She stood leaning against the bar, drained, angry, guilty, embarrassed. Without looking at Daniel she spoke, "I'm sorry you heard that."

Daniel came up behind her and put his hands on her shoulders. It seemed the most natural thing in the world to turn into his arms.

His voice was a soft whisper in her ear. "*You're* sorry? I promise never to let you forget to call again."

Annie stood in the shelter of his arms, not hugging him back, just enjoying the sensation of being cared for. It was wonderful, having someone offer comfort without demands. With his arms around her and the perfect spot to rest her head, she would have been content to stay put all evening and let the tension, anger and guilt drain away.

"You're right, you know, you're absolutely right about one thing. There are times when my parents just won't give me any breathing room." She was mumbling into the wool of Daniel's vest. She wasn't even sure he could hear it.

He heard the last few words and slid his hands down her arms, taking her hands in his. Did she know she had tears in her eyes? She might say she was committed to her family, but *trapped* would be a better word. He wondered if the thought had ever occurred to her. It might not have occurred to him, either, if he hadn't seen the pain in her eyes.

He led her to the couch and sat next to her, holding Annie's hand lightly, to give her reassurance. He hoped maybe a little of her openness would flow between them. He wasn't used to sharing feelings. It was almost as risky as testing a rope bridge for the first time.

"Annie, honey, I know you didn't want to hear this an hour ago, but it has to be said." He took a deep breath and moved a little closer. "It's about families, about parents and how they're supposed to help you grow, not hold you back. The thing is, there's a difference between love and possession. I'm not sure that's something your family realizes.

"Do you think it was easy for my parents to let us leave every Christmas? Mom would cry and Dad would finger his handkerchief the whole time we were at the airport. But they thought it was important for us to gain that little independence. Dad always said that a family grounded in love would be together no matter how far apart they were.

"When they died and I spent all those hours on the plane over and back that phrase was like a mantra to me. So now, even though they're dead, I still have their love. It's almost as good as having them."

He wanted to kiss away the tears that she was trying so hard to restrain. He knew she understood. He just wasn't sure she was willing to accept it.

"Your parents are doing their best to tie you down with guilt, with responsibilities, with a kind of love that's selfish and destructive. Believe me, that's not the way it's supposed to be.

"Their motives might be the best in the world. To keep you safe, to spare you pain, but the fact is they can't protect you from life." He had a hard time seeing the Ver-Hollans as anything but selfish, but he wouldn't go any distance in convincing Annie if he didn't make their possessiveness a little more palatable.

Annie pulled her hand away and edged back into the corner of the small love seat. "I guess my parents *can* seem possessive. I'd be lying if I insisted they never got on my nerves. But I'm not so sure your upbringing was the best, either. Every family's different, that's all. Sure, your family encouraged independence and look what that cost you."

"My family did encourage independence, but the mistakes were all mine. My folks put me on the right path and let me learn from my own experience. I was the one that blew it, not them."

He moved closer again, not wanting to lose the concession she'd just made. If he sat close and held her hand, he knew they wouldn't argue—arguing was the last thing he thought about when he was this close to her. He was overwhelmed with the need to free her, to see her smile, to make her happy.

He could feel the pulse in her wrist, throbbing a delicate rhythm, each tiny beat echoing through his body. Pulling her close with an arm around her shoulders, he raised her chin with his hand until they were face-to-face.

"It's so rare that you don't smile. And you were so happy before that silly phone call."

She shook her head and closed her eyes. "I feel like it's been a hundred years since I had something to smile about."

"Can I help?" He touched his lips to hers in the gentlest of caresses. An explosion of sensation raced through him and all thoughts of consolation were obliterated. He wanted to mold her body to his, savor the feel of her warmth and welcome. Instead his lips held hers, capturing her mouth in a dozen little kisses, each one beginning, promising, asking, teasing. He felt her hesitate, then her reserve melted away. Annie molded her mouth to each touch, her response still more tentative than his. Did she feel the same longing?

He kissed the corner of her mouth. He gave one last caress to the sweet curve of her neck. Daniel drew back slightly and Annie smiled. "That helped a lot," she whispered.

He pulled her into the curve of his arm and pressed a kiss on her temple. The sweet smell of her skin, the softness of her hair so close drew a deep, shuddering sigh from him so that Annie turned slightly. "Are you okay?"

He nodded and nestled her close for a moment more. God knows, he'd shared more of himself with Annie in the past few minutes than he'd ever shared with anyone before in his life. He hadn't even been sure why. At first he'd thought it was because it would be too selfish to claim his children and not leave some future for her.

He hadn't really understood his motivation until he kissed her. And then he knew quite simply. He loved her too much to leave her with nothing.

Chapter Seven

Daddy, it was so much fun. They had a whole spaceship made of Legos—one you could walk into! How many Legos do you think it took to make something that big?" Kendall bounced on the bed, while Jessica answered her sister's question.

"Millions, I think."

Annie leaned closer and whispered, "If you were looking for a little quiet bedtime conversation, I think you brought up the wrong subject." Daniel and Annie were sharing the bedtime ritual for the first time. He liked the feel of it, the sharing and the closeness.

Daniel nodded and turned to his two gymnasts. "Now, listen you two, it's time to settle down. If you can't talk about your adventure without treating the bed like a trampoline, then maybe we'd better skip this and turn out the light." The threat didn't work until he took Annie's hand and began to rise from the edge of the bed.

Kendall and Jessica looked at each other and immediately stopped shaking the springs. They scrambled under the covers and looked so angelic that both Daniel and Annie laughed.

Daniel nodded his approval. "Well, I'm glad you got the message. Now why don't we both read you that next chapter of *The Little Princess*."

"Okay," Kendall agreed. "You can be the man parts and Annie can be the girl parts."

Daniel smiled at the girls and the woman beside him. "I wouldn't have it any other way."

Annie definitely had the larger part. He sat back, listening to her sweet Southern voice and let the drawl sweep over him. The slow, soft cadence touched his heart as completely as her tears had a few hours ago. Her voice reminded him of the welcoming warmth of her lips when he'd kissed her, when he'd realized he loved her.

They smiled at each other as Annie showed the girls an illustration. He had no doubts. He did love her, in a hundred different ways. The way she talked, and smiled. He even loved the way she sipped tea, all curled up on the couch like a kitten.

"Daddy, you're not paying attention." Kendall distracted him and he turned promptly to his single line.

Annie smiled at him, he smiled back. As she turned the page she whispered, "You don't have many lines, but they're very important."

He nodded solemnly and promptly lost himself in her voice again.

She was teasing him, but she'd never spoken truer words. He hadn't played any part in the twins' lives until the last two years, but even though his part had been small, she'd made him appreciate how important he had been and would always be. If he loved her in a hundred different ways, then it was also true he loved her for a hundred different reasons. That was only one of them.

He almost missed his next line and forced himself to pay attention until the final phrase was read. They spent a minute or two discussing the ending, then Annie suggested prayers.

"Can we say them to ourselves tonight? I'm praying for something that's a secret." Kendall smiled at Jessica who nodded vigorously. Apparently it was only a secret from him and Annie.

Annie was called away by a telephone call and Daniel sat while the girls lay with eyes closed and hands folded. He had a few prayers himself. He knew he would need some significant outside help over the next few months, putting his life in order, adjusting to his role as father, getting Annie to accept just how important she was to him, figuring out exactly what their future together was.

It wasn't difficult to imagine her as a permanent part of his life when she was in his arms, capturing him in a kaleidoscope of feelings. He held on to the thought and hoped that the practical details wouldn't shatter the dream.

There was a dull gray cast to the morning light that almost convinced Annie her clock was wrong. It was so quiet. No police sirens, no garbage trucks, even the sounds of traffic were muted. She summoned all her energy and lifted her head to check the time again. It still read just a little past seven-thirty. Should she get up? She didn't hear any sounds beyond her room. Wouldn't it be nice if everyone was sleeping in? This was vacation, wasn't it? With an indulgent sigh, she settled back on her pillow and nestled under the covers.

Besides, she had a lot to think about. Her feelings were a jumble and she wanted to resolve them before she saw Daniel again. Things had changed between them and she wasn't sure if she was glad or not.

How could a little kiss cause such turmoil? Heaven knew she'd needed a dose of tender care after that phone conversation with her mother. She smiled. Daniel had been there for her and it was a wonderful feeling. He'd known just what to do. He'd hugged her, dried her tears. He'd shared feelings with a wisdom that had presented her with a whole new perspective. He'd kissed her. She hadn't felt a moment's hesitation then, only a sense of comfort, of belonging.

So why did she feel so confused now?

There was one obvious explanation. She felt guilty because Daniel was Kathy's husband. But that really wasn't true. It hadn't been true for six years. Annie tried, but couldn't summon the least bit of guilt on that score.

A wave of grief clutched at her, a random blow of pain, because Kathy was gone and the world had changed. Why had her sister been killed and two beautiful children left motherless? Why hadn't she been the one driving to the grocery store that day?

That sense of loss, even guilt, had nothing to do with Daniel, or with their kiss. Kathy might think she was crazy to be intrigued by Daniel Marshall, but she wouldn't be jealous.

And Annie *was* intrigued. The surge of tears disappeared with the thought. Annie hugged her pillow tighter and confronted the truth.

There had been more than comfort in that kiss. There had been passion, too. A passion so real that even now, recalling the kiss, an echo of desire swept through her. Their embrace had stirred a whole new range of emotions; was a catalyst for a whole new relationship.

All her confusion evaporated at the admission.

Annie turned onto her back, put her hands behind her head and considered yesterday afternoon and evening in the light of the new insight. Was she overanalyzing or had the few hours between the girls' return and bedtime been filled with subtle little changes that were sure evidence that Daniel cared, too? For the first time she and Daniel sat next to each other at dinner, with the girls across from them. It wasn't much, but now, looking back on it, there was an implied partnership in the arrangement. They weren't confronting each other anymore.

Daniel had found excuses to take her arm, to touch her, to whisper in her ear. None of the gestures had been loverlike, but spoke of a communication more meaningful than what they'd had before.

They'd even shared the girls' bedtime ritual. Nothing monumental, but a number of little things that surely altered the pattern of their relationship. Each one of those innocent exchanges had made Annie more and more aware of Daniel as a man.

For a moment she smiled, savoring the thought, the exhilaration. It was a heady feeling to share so strong an attraction.

Exhilaration gave way to reality.

Was it wise? Was it fair to let their attraction draw them toward a more intimate relationship? Weren't the girls the focal point of their lives? She had a responsibility to the twins, and to her parents. How could she let her feelings destroy the stability she'd worked so hard to develop over the past two years? Wouldn't it be infinitely wiser to build on the friendship and forget the desire?

But could she settle for friendship?

It wouldn't be easy to bury the longing and build on more passive feelings. But it would be easier if she did it now, before either one of them gave voice to their thoughts. It wasn't what she wanted. It wasn't what she wanted at all. But hadn't she learned long ago that what she wanted and what was best are sometimes two different things?

The sacrifice would be a fair trade. Surely she could renounce the attraction in exchange for friendship and an end to the tension that had marked their first week together, the reserve that had undercut all their correspondence and their few phone conversations.

Weeks, maybe even years of anxiety were gone. Friendship would make life so easy, would smooth over a hundred of their previous conflicts. When Daniel went back to Africa or on to a new post, friendship would keep the communication open. Maybe she and the girls could visit him. She would love to see where he lived, meet his friends, see his projects, just spend time together.

The lightest of taps on the door drew her attention. Annie sat up in bed and called, "Come in."

Daniel eased the door open and leaned around it. "Good morning," he whispered. His words were accompanied by such a roguish smile that Annie was sure of two things. It wouldn't be easy to defuse the attraction, but friendship was definitely the wisest course.

"Look out your window." Without further comment he closed the door.

Annie grabbed her robe from the foot of the bed. The room was chilly and she held the lightweight material tightly to ward off the cold. At first she thought the window was fogged over. Then she realized that her view was blurred by a blanket of snow that had fallen during the night and continued even now.

The snowflakes were as effective as any cup of coffee. She hurried to the door and found Daniel across the room watching the view from the double window in the living room of the suite. He turned toward her.

"It's wonderful."

Daniel nodded in agreement and Annie came to admire the landscape from his window. They stood silent a moment watching the snow change the landscape.

Annie whispered. "It's so quiet. I guess that's what woke me up. I didn't hear any of the usual city noises. The snow muffles everything."

The cold penetrated the glass and Annie shivered. Daniel put an arm around her and gave her shoulder a squeeze.

She resisted the urge to lay her head on his shoulder, but rejected the wisdom of stepping away from the casual embrace. One last moment, she thought.

She stared out the window and tried to memorize the way his body felt pressed next to hers—strong, warm, vital. This would be one of her treasured memories, this brief moment standing together, watching the morning unfold.

"When was the last time you saw snow?" She turned her head and inhaled the woodsy scent of his after-shave, admired the curve of his chin and stepped out of the embrace, resisting the magnetism that pulled her.

She drew on her resolve and changed her perspective. Last night's whispering and hand-holding had been just part of a holiday-induced euphoria, nothing more. How incredibly juvenile to read more than that into a casual gesture of affection.

She was fully prepared to deny the truth.

Daniel was standing alone at the window now, but he was watching Annie, not the snow. "Must be all of five years since I've seen any at all."

"It hasn't been that long for me. But we never get any snow that stays longer than twenty-four hours." Annie chattered on. "Won't the girls love this? There's something so special about an unexpected snowfall. It's like an invitation to take the day off, to come out and play, be a kid again."

"Annie! Daddy! Do you see the snow? Can we go out?" Kendall and Jessica came racing out of their room, half dressed and already pulling on their snow pants.

It was the only invitation Annie needed. She'd already spent entirely too much time dissecting an incident. "I was just going to come and wake you two sleepyheads up."

Kendall tugged her hand. "Let's hurry, Annie. Before the snow melts!" With that fear as incentive, the foursome were suited up and ready for the elements before the first plow was on the street.

The girls were all smiles and excitement, eager to hurry to the park. Daniel seemed preoccupied, but in good spirits, too. When they reached the lobby he shooed them out the door.

"Go on ahead, Annie. There's something I want to take care of before I join you." He thought a moment. "Would you wait for me at the park entrance?"

Annie wanted to question him, but thought better of it. It was Christmas, after all. Everyone was entitled to a secret or two.

As they trooped crosstown toward Central Park, Annie followed the twins who raced ahead. They kicked drifts of snow and slid on the slight sheen of ice beneath the powder. She smiled out of habit and affection. But she was too mired in her own thoughts to share their excitement.

This friendship ploy—the denial of attraction—would bring a tension all its own. Maybe they hadn't vocalized their feelings, but they'd surely communicated them in a hundred more basic ways. Annie sighed. It would have to be that same basic communication that got the new message across. *We're meant for nothing more than friendship.*

Kendall's clumsily thrown snowball hit her on the leg. "Come on, Annie," she called, "we want to play!" It was hard to think about anything serious with two such enthusiastic snow bunnies. She tossed a badly aimed snowball in their direction and then raced them to the park entrance.

Even the continuing snowfall wasn't enough to dampen the hoots and shouts of groups swooping down the hilly terrain. Adults stood in clusters watching children, waiting for them to tire, so they could have their turn. Parents and children rode sleds together, ending in laughing heaps at the bottom of the hills where snow had drifted.

Just as Annie was beginning to wonder where they could find sleds for the girls, Daniel arrived. He carried two large round plastic serving trays, the kind the waiters used for room service. "Oh, Daniel, you found sleds!" Annie was definitely impressed with his ingenuity.

"Hey, one thing I've learned to do is improvise."

"I guess I shouldn't ask exactly how you got them."

"It's between me and the bell captain."

They turned their attention to the park, searching for Kendall and Jessica, who'd found a whopper of a sledding hill and were watching with undisguised envy.

"Somehow, I don't think your daughters are going to give a thought to whether you got these by fair means or foul." Annie took one of the sleds. It wasn't that Daniel needed help. But carrying the large tray was a convenient way to avoid holding his hand.

"Daniel, look at all the people here. It can't always be this full of activity."

He stopped behind her and she felt his hand on her shoulder. She stepped away and softened the rejection with a smile, a nice friendly smile.

He looked puzzled and was about to give voice to the thought. Annie rushed into speech, "Look at the snow on the trees. It looks like one of those Christmas-card landscapes, doesn't it?"

He nodded, still puzzled, but followed her train of thought, "And definitely not the peaceful, tranquil kind."

As Annie had predicted, the girls had no questions about the whys or hows of the sled acquisition. Kendall grabbed her sled and handed one to Jessica. "We're going down the biggest hill!"

Daniel stopped her with a firm hand on the shoulder. "Young lady, you two start on that slope over there." He pointed to a slope where mothers and babies were inching down a gentle incline. "Once you've got the hang of it you can move on to something tougher."

There were a few other adults standing nearby, supervising youngsters, and one mother smiled at the girl's grudging acceptance of Daniel's decision. She turned to Annie. "Looks like you've got a daredevil on your hands."

Annie walked closer, glad for an excuse to avoid one-on-one conversation with Daniel. "That and she thinks she's the one in charge most of the time." Annie looked around. "Which ones are yours?"

The woman pointed out a man and baby riding down the hill. "I've only got one. My husband has him on the sled. Actually, Rob's dying to try the big hill, but we only have one sled. So he has to wait until Benjy gets tired."

Daniel joined them then and Annie included him in the conversation. The three chatted, watching the hill the whole time. It was pleasantly impersonal, just as Annie had hoped. Once she caught a speculative glance Daniel shot at her. She knew he was puzzled, but decided that actions spoke louder than words. She ignored the unspoken question and pointed toward the girls, "Don't you think they're ready for something a little more challenging?"

Daniel watched as the girls made a run down the slope. Kendall looked disgusted and even Jessica seemed bored. "I guess you're right."

"I bet you're as anxious as Rob over there to try the big hill. How about if we go down with them? Then they'll have some on-site adult supervision." Annie congratulated herself on her cleverness. Riding on different sleds would preclude even the most trivial conversation.

The sleds weren't nearly as efficient with the heavier load, but it didn't diminish the girls' enthusiasm. They'd made four runs when they met at the bottom of the hill. Daniel grabbed Annie's hand and spoke to Jessica, "How about if Annie and I go down together?"

In a gesture of panicked inspiration, Annie pulled Daniel's hand as hard as she could and pushed him into a snowbank. The idea of a snow fight appealed to Kendall and Jessica who jumped on Annie and knocked her down, as well.

It was a storybook day. Sometime after noon they realized they were starving. Daniel suggested hot dogs and hot chocolate from one of the vendors just outside the park. Then Annie thought of building a snowman.

Everything would be fine, she decided. They could be friends; she wanted them to be friends. Reminding herself that Kendall and Jessica were the foundation of their relationship was enough to help her keep the proper perspective.

"Over here, Annie." She looked toward Jessica's voice. While she was lost in thought the rest of them had found a level spot.

Daniel walked toward her. "The snow's still coming down and there's already plenty here to work with. Let's you and me enjoy the show."

"No way, Daniel. I hardly ever get a chance to build a snowman."

The second giant snowball was completed before Kendall noted her father's absence. "Come on, Daddy," Kendall called. "You have to help, too."

Daniel walked over and did some calculation with his hands. "Now I don't mean to be a party pooper, but as an experienced site supervisor, I can tell you you're going to need a crane to get the body on the base."

With a groan, the three acknowledged the truth of his assessment. Annie stepped back and viewed the giant snowball from Daniel's perspective. "Good heavens, girls, your dad's right. Frosty's base is almost as tall as you two. There's no way we can get the second snowball on top."

"What if we get some help?" Already Kendall was scanning the area for assistance. But the crowd had thinned considerably. The closest help was some distance away.

"No, honey," Annie answered. "I don't think that will work, either. I guess we just have to start over."

"I know, Daddy. You and Annie build the snowman. Jessica and I will be the ones in charge. We'll sit right here." Kendall proceeded to carve seats out of the large base they'd rolled and gestured for Annie and Daniel to get to work.

Annie leaned toward Daniel. "I guess there's a bit of her dad in her. What was that term?" She tapped her hand on her mouth in thought, "Ah yes, 'site supervisor.' Do you think Kendall has what it takes?"

"Come on, Daddy. Stop talking. It's getting cold just sitting here."

Daniel looked at Annie with raised eyebrows. "Maybe we should form a union. That girl can be a real taskmaster."

Under the girls' direct scrutiny the snowman took shape, but soon they were complaining of the cold in earnest. Annie encouraged them to take their "sleds" out on the hill again.

It was fun working with Daniel, even on something as inconsequential as a snowman. The two of them huffed and puffed as they lifted the body onto the base. The head was easy. Even though Frosty had a distinct bend to the left, he was theirs and Annie and Daniel stepped back to admire his blue cap, borrowed from Annie and his red muffler, Daniel's contribution.

When Daniel reached for her hand, Annie hurried to retie the scarf and then looked away from him, watching the girls. Daniel walked up beside her and turned her to face him. He was holding her hat.

"Here, I really think you need this more than Frosty." He put the hat on her head and framed her face with his hands.

Annie tried to ignore the flutter of feeling that tickled her heart and settled as a dull ache. "Oh, let the girls see it on him." Her words faded as Daniel didn't move away.

"Honey, the girls have already forgotten about our snowman. Seems to me you've forgotten something, too. Could it be you just need a little reminder?"

As she smiled and leaned into the kiss Annie decided this would be as good a time as any to prove to him that all she had in mind was friendship.

His lips met hers, warm and wanting. There was such an aching hunger in his touch that Annie lost all sense of her purpose and wreathed her arms around his neck, pressing closer. The dull ache that had settled around her heart now warmed her whole body. Daniel's lips were a stirring persuasion, a sweet demand.

The layers of clothes that insulated them left only their mouths to communicate. Annie opened her mouth to his and their kiss deepened, Daniel's tongue tasting, touching, tracing a path of sensuous pleasure that left Annie breathless.

Friendship was an admirable goal. She sought it for all the right reasons, but the passion that lay just below the surface wouldn't go away. They would have to deal with it, just as they had dealt with the hundred other issues that had clouded their relationship. Somehow she was going to have to convince Daniel that friendship was the only realistic possibility. She ignored the fact that first she would have to convince herself.

Still in his arms, she raised her eyes to him. "Daniel, we have to talk about this."

He smiled. It was a genuine heart-stopping grin—so rare for Daniel that Annie wondered how much true happiness he'd known in his life. "Annie, darling, why do you think talking will resolve everything? The truth is, words couldn't begin to describe that kiss or the way it made us feel. I'm not sure I even want to try."

Annie shrugged.

He took her hand and pulled her toward the sledding hill. "Don't you think those girls need a nap? Let's find them, feed them and settle them down. Then you and I can talk if that's what you'd *really* rather do."

Chapter Eight

Annie curled up on the bed and settled against the pillows. She hadn't talked to Mary Jane since she'd left Avon. Annie decided this phone call was a Christmas present to herself. "So how's Roy?"

"Oh, honestly, Annie, the man is such a jerk. He refuses to even consider changing the Christmas routine: you know, Christmas Eve at his house and Christmas Day at mine. I want to be there when my nieces and nephews open their presents, but he says we have to honor tradition. He can't understand why my folks have suddenly decided to open presents on Christmas Eve instead of Christmas Day. I ask you, how can I possibly love someone who makes me this mad?"

Annie understood perfectly. But despite the misunderstanding between her and Daniel, Annie felt none of the deep-seated frustration she heard in Mary Jane's voice. "You've known each other for twenty years. If you didn't love him, don't you think you'd know by now?"

"Time has nothing to do with it, Annie. I'm convinced that loving someone is something you know instinctively. And my instincts are telling me I'm about to make a big mistake."

"You mean the ring?"

"I surely do. He keeps hinting and Mr. Thornton at the jewelry store told Mother that Roy brought his grandmother's ring in to be cleaned. What does that sound like to you?"

"Sounds like it's decision time."

"Honestly, Annie, I like him. I always have—even when we spend hours bickering over whether to watch football or go to a movie. That's okay after twenty years of marriage, but not before the honeymoon. What am I talking about? We're not even engaged!"

"MJ, you're telling me there's no spark when he kisses you?"

"None."

Annie thought about the way she felt when Daniel held her hand. "His touch doesn't make you forget practical and think physical?"

"Are you kidding?"

Annie smiled, thinking about the first kiss she'd shared with Daniel. "You two don't help each other over the rough spots?"

"Annie, he *is* the rough spot. The other day..."

Annie nodded and listened. It sounded as if Mary Jane and Roy had the makings of a beautiful friendship. But as the conversation with Mary Jane unfolded, Annie was convinced that simple friendship between her and Daniel was impossible. The instinctive knowledge Mary Jane mentioned was already a fact. Had it been there all those years ago when they first met? Was that why she'd disliked him so much at first? Had it been a sort of defense mechanism against the chemistry that she now accepted? As a teenager, such feelings could be confusing, but at twenty-four she hoped she was more in touch with her emotions.

"That's enough about me and Roy. Tell me, how are things going with you? Is your mother calling every day?"

"Just about. I called her before I called you and she actually seems to have mellowed a little. She didn't accuse Daniel of any grim intent and told me she had a good time at the Bennetts' party. Last week she'd insisted she wouldn't enjoy one single moment of the holidays."

"I saw her at the grocery store just two days ago and even though she was dressed in black, I did get her to smile and she even agreed to come to the school open house. I bribed her by telling her that Jessica had three paintings on display." Mary Jane paused a moment. "And what about Daniel? Are you being civil to each other yet?"

She and Daniel were way beyond that and there was no chance to backtrack, but this didn't seem like the best time to bring the subject up. Someday she would have to tell Mary Jane exactly how much her confusion had helped Annie to resolve her own.

"Everything's fine here. The girls are having a wonderful time." She paused for a moment, searching for a suitably honest but neutral description. "I'm having a wonderful time, too."

"That sounds pretty positive. So Daniel's not such a bad guy, after all?"

He's wonderful, Annie thought. "No, he's not. I think for the first time I've realized that it takes two people to make a marriage fail."

"Wow, Annie. I never thought I'd hear that from a VerHollan. The guy must be pretty convincing."

Annie shrugged. "I guess he is, and it's so obvious he cares about the girls. I just never understood how much. In the last few days he's been a model father."

She gave Mary Jane a routine description of their holiday, still avoiding any indication of the change in her relationship with Daniel. She wasn't going to say a word until she knew if they had a future.

"Okay, Annie, suppose you tell me exactly what's bothering you?" Daniel sat down beside her on the love seat where she was nursing a cup of tea. He patted his pocket, looking for his pipe, then once again remembered he'd left it behind. It was at times like these that he missed it.

She turned to him with a wistful smile. "I just don't know what to do. You see—" her voice dropped to a confidential whisper and the smile grew "—I'm wildly attracted to this wonderful man and it just won't work at all."

Her smile faded with the admission. It was replaced by a look of such disappointment that Daniel had to fight the urge to take her in his arms. He knew he could kiss away her doubts, but he wanted more than that. So instead of an embrace, he took her cup of tea, set it on the table and took her hand. "And why do you think 'it won't work at all'?"

"How can it? We've been all but enemies for so long. How can we go from that to being more than friends? Shouldn't friendship be enough?"

"Is that what you want?" He still resisted the urge to move closer, but his eyes held hers. *The truth, Annie.*

She looked away, then down at her hands briefly. "Surely, it's what's best for everyone concerned." Then she looked at him again and spoke in a rush, "But, to be honest, I want to be in your arms and let the world take care of itself."

Annie stood up and moved away from the love seat as if she were afraid that Daniel would grant her wish.

"So why can't we let that happen?" He stood up and walked toward her, aching with the need to show her how easy it was to communicate without words.

"There are other things that come first. I have responsibilities. And so do you."

Daniel stopped a few feet away. Ah, yes, responsibilities. He bristled at the word, in fact, he hated it. It was the Verhollans' catchphrase, the word they used to recall all those parental urgings to put family first.

He looked at Annie who was watching him with arms folded, in a stance so defensive, he knew they were a breath away from an argument. Once before, Annie had wanted to avoid an argument at all costs. He understood that feeling now. What she was saying, what he wanted her to understand, was too important to be detoured by a heated exchange.

He wanted to understand her. Why was she afraid?

"Yes, I know we both have responsibilities. What makes you think our responsibilities and our, um, attraction are mutually exclusive?"

"It's just that it complicates things so much. What happens when you leave, when I go back to Avon? What happens when you get a new job? What happens when—"

"I take the girls? What happens when... Annie, that kind of 'what if' could go on forever."

He stepped closer, certain he could convince her that the present was what mattered and future would resolve itself. "Are you really that afraid of the unknown? Is this the same woman who talked so longingly of joining the Peace Corps?"

Annie finally looked him in the eye and smiled a little. "Do I really sound like that much of a coward?"

He shook his head. "Not a coward, but the truth is, you sound entirely too timid for the Annie VerHollan I've gotten to know. Can't you look on this as a great adventure? We don't know how it will turn out, but isn't that the way it is with all the best adventures?"

He moved closer and gathered her into his arms. Daniel meant the kiss as a gentle persuasion. His lips touched hers with a lingering tenderness that grew sweeter and sweeter in its sensual demand. His kiss was a seal, a promise, a vow that for all the adventure he promised they would go carefully. They might not have much time tonight, but the future stretched before them, promising endless days and nights. He wouldn't crowd her now; they had the luxury of tomorrow.

Annie returned the kiss. All the openness and giving that were essential to her was in her response. There was more than tenderness. There was a wild excitement that arced between them, transmitted by a touch. Daniel promised tenderness, but he welcomed the excitement.

He held her close, his hands molding her to him, this time promising intimacy, arousal and fulfillment. He wanted to give her some taste of the pleasure to come. He wanted to feel her soft and eager, the warmth of her body wanting him. But he wanted more than that. He wanted the right moment, the right time—not an impulsive act that she might come to regret.

He eased his hold, caressing her face, moving a fraction away from the edge of desire. They stood close together for a moment longer, sharing the promise. Daniel pressed her head to his shoulder and kissed her hair just as a familiar knock sounded.

Annie raised her head and eased herself out of Daniel's arms. "Were you expecting Davis?"

Daniel nodded. "I called him this morning. I can't say I would have minded if he'd arrived a little later."

Davis knocked again. "But I guess he won't go away." The two shared shrugs of resignation and opened the door to the ebullient Marshall.

A giant Christmas tree filled the doorway, a long-needled pine, flocked a snowy white on the tips. It was an artificial tree, but still the room was filled with the smell of pine as Davis pushed the tree in ahead of him.

"Look what I found in the hall. And it has your name on it."

The threesome spent the next twenty minutes discussing exact placement. By the time they were done, the twins had been roused from their nap and were anxious to decorate the tree.

Davis scooped Jessica into his arms and grabbed Kendall's hand. "First the three of us have to buy the lights and ornaments. And we don't have much time if we want to do that and have dinner, too."

The girls were dressed and ready for the outing before the naptime flush had faded from their cheeks. Annie worried about the streets in the aftermath of the storm, but Davis assured her the main roads were passable.

Davis turned back one last time and Daniel wondered exactly what he'd planned for them this time. "The only thing you two have to find is the ornament for the top of the tree. We'll be back before bedtime."

The door closed on three excited voices. Annie looked at Daniel. "Exactly what time do you think Davis considers 'bedtime'?"

"I hate to even guess. But it may take us that long to search out our part of the tree decor."

Annie ran to the closet and pulled out his coat. "I told you all that shopping would come in handy. I know exactly what I want for the top of the tree." She threw Daniel his gloves. "What's more, I know exactly where to find it."

Grabbing the rest of their cold-weather wear, they rushed from the hotel, grabbed a cab and made it to the Metropolitan Museum of Art just before it closed.

Daniel followed her up the steps toward the entrance. "Annie, I thought when that million dollar check bounced I'd convinced you I wasn't made of money. Besides, I don't think the artwork here is for sale."

Annie scooped up a soggy handful of snow and tossed it his way.

The entry hall was bustling with visitors. The enthusiasm of all those art lovers was contagious. Annie, Daniel and the girls had visited the museum briefly days ago, but the girls' endurance had been limited. Now Daniel suggested they take another look around.

Annie discouraged the idea. "You know how big this place is. Even a quick look around would take hours." She glanced at her watch. "And we have exactly twenty minutes until it closes."

Daniel acquiesced but only after he insisted, "You have to promise this will be our first stop the next time we come to New York."

Annie smiled and agreed, pulling him toward the gift shop. His words echoed through her mind. The simple statement filled her with promise, and a dash of hope. He talked about the future with such easy assurance that she almost believed they had one.

The shop was bursting with shoppers and Daniel pulled her back from the entrance. "This place is entirely too crowded for me."

Annie pulled him forward. "Come on, I know exactly what I want and where it is." He still resisted. "Daniel, we're creating a tradition here. It really needs your approval." She was perfectly serious. Daniel leaned forward and kissed a smile on her lips.

They walked into the shop together. He held her hand as they moved through the raft of shoppers. "Are you sure this little item is good enough to sit on the Marshall Christmas tree for years?"

Annie shrugged. "Just wait and see."

The clerk pulled the sample out of the case so Daniel could get a closer look.

Annie began her sales pitch, "It's a replica of the angels that are on the Christmas tree we saw here the other day."

Daniel turned the delicate piece over, examining it carefully. It was a Renaissance beauty, about eighteen inches high with flowing robes of rose and gold.

He handed the angel to the clerk with a nod and then turned to Annie. "It's absolutely beautiful," he said with a smile. "And it reminds me of you."

Annie blushed at the absurd compliment. "Surely it's worthy of the tradition."

Daniel nodded, as serious now as she'd been earlier. Annie watched him as he went through the routine of paying the clerk and accepting the carefully wrapped package. She could visualize him unwrapping it. As the years passed, Daniel would take his angel out of its delicate tissue wrapping and unwrap a lifetime of memories along with it. Would they be happy ones?

They moved away from the crowd around the register. Daniel tucked her arm through his and then leaned closer. "You're too serious. No solemn looks allowed."

She looked at him and a small smile escaped.

"Every time I see you frown I'm going to have to take some serious remedial action." He accompanied the words with a smile of his own.

Annie laughed at his phrasing, then tried to frown to test the retribution. She pursed her lips but the edges still curved up. She bit the inside of her lip, but her eyes still twinkled. Finally she gave up and accepted the fact that the day was made for smiling.

The line for available cabs was monstrous, so Annie and Daniel decided to take the bus down Fifth Avenue. That bit of practicality didn't last long. They got as far as the edge of Central Park near the Plaza Hotel when Daniel grabbed Annie's hand. "How about a horse-drawn cab?"

A horse? Daniel wanted to ride behind a horse? They were off the bus and Daniel was bargaining with the driver before Annie was sure of exactly what he meant. A moment later they were in the horse-drawn buggy, headed through Central Park in the last of the twilight.

The snow had stopped hours before and the streets were little more than a slushy mess. The temperature hovered around freezing, however, so the snow still clung to tree limbs and rocks, giving the park an ethereal appearance.

They didn't say anything at first. The hooded cab reduced the cold and the wool blanket the driver provided helped them stay warm, but the two couldn't resist the excuse to sit close, fingers entwined. Annie listened to the rhythmic hollow chock of the horse's hooves.

It was Daniel who broke the silence. "I've always wondered about one little innocuous thing."

Annie rested her head on Daniel's shoulder and decided it probably wasn't little or innocuous. "And what was that?"

"The letters you wrote. They meant so much to me. I used to read them until they were worn thin. I remember every word you wrote, the stray cats they brought home, the first time they tied their shoes."

Annie treasured the words. This was a kind of "true confession" she could handle. She moved a little closer and turned to face him. "I had to admit it got so Thursday was my favorite day. Your letter would arrive and it would kill me to have to wait until Kendall and Jessica got home. After all, it was addressed to them."

"There was always one thing I wondered about."

They were a breath apart.

"What's that?" Annie whispered.

"How come you never once closed with anything more than your name?"

"What do you think I should have put?" She was teasing him now. Two could play this game.

"You could have put, 'sincerely,' or 'regards' or 'fondly,' or..."

He paused and Annie filled in the blank just before she kissed him. "Or maybe I could have put 'love.'"

It was the first kiss she had initiated and she reveled in the pleasure of it. His lips were cool, but warmed quickly as she pressed simple kisses and then fit her mouth to his in a heady exploration that left them both breathless and oblivious to their surroundings.

Her tongue met his in an intimate expression of promised passion, the sensual demand an echo of the longing that held them in the embrace. The cab rocked around a corner and moved out of the park. The kiss ended abruptly, as the life of the city street destroyed the moment.

The driver dropped them a block or two away from the Hard Rock Cafe. But it was too noisy and crowded to suit their mood. They walked a bit more and found The Manhattan Ocean Club. It came highly recommended by their concierge and they were early enough so seating wasn't a problem.

The decor was crisply modern—clean lines with railings and a mezzanine that conveyed the feel of a cruise ship. The food was wonderful, their waiter unobtrusive.

They both ordered lobster bisque as a first course. Annie decided on salmon, Daniel wanted oysters, but they were unavailable, so he opted for red snapper instead. They chose a wine with the help of the sommelier and sipped it while they waited for their first course.

Food had never seemed so seductive or eating quite so sensuous before. The lobster bisque was peppery and smooth with a hint of nutmeg. It was served in small, covered bowls. Annie sipped her wine and watched Daniel's hands as he spooned the soup. They were competent hands, strong and slender. She wanted to feel those hands on her. She watched as he lifted the spoon to his mouth and wanted to taste his lips, still warm with a hint of spice and sherry.

Hours later, as they wandered back toward the hotel, halfheartedly looking for a cab, Annie tried to remember what they had talked about—a few casual comments about a number of inconsequential things. Most of their conversation had ended in a grin or a look that made words unnecessary.

Tonight was all that had meaning. This was one evening out of a lifetime when the past didn't matter and the future was found in the promise of the present. They walked hand in hand up Fifth Avenue and every glittering star, whether fashioned by man or Mother Nature, shimmered just for them. They walked on, and Annie willed the moment to last forever.

"Doesn't the tree look great, Jessica?" Annie threaded a hook on the last ornament and handed it to her niece. They both turned toward the tree; Jessica moved closer to the branches, considering each vacant spot. From where she sat on the floor, Annie watched her niece, her heart wrung with such love and hope that a rush of tears filled her eyes.

"Is here good, Annie?" Jessica turned and waited for approval.

Annie sniffed away the emotion and smiled. "That's a perfect spot, sweetheart."

Empty boxes, tissue paper and shopping bags—a testament to their activity—littered the living area. Annie began to gather the containers and stuff them carefully into the largest bag. They would need them when the time came to dismantle the tree. Her movements were automatic, her thoughts centered on the thousand sentimental memories that had crowded her mind all day.

She remembered Kendall and Jessica's first Christmas. They'd only been a few months old, but her family, the whole neighborhood, had made such a fuss. She wished she'd thought to bring pictures so Daniel could share the recollection.

Their last year in nursery school they'd been reindeer in the live tableau at city hall. She'd passed on the reindeer costumes to the next year's cast, but Daniel would have enjoyed the newspaper clippings if she had thought to bring them.

Annie watched as Kendall directed the placement of the ornaments on the upper branches. Her directions were imperious and her patience limited.

"No, Daddy, not that branch, the one two branches higher, near the red light."

Daniel followed the order and when Kendall turned to ask her aunt if there were any more ornaments, Daniel caught Annie's eye and he raised his eyebrows in amused exasperation. She could almost read his mind. *Must be a VerHollan trait. No Marshall was ever this picky about a Christmas tree.* Her melancholy disappeared. She gave him an encouraging thumbs-up and a smile.

They'd saved the special treetop ornament for last. Daniel stayed on the chair he was using as a ladder and waited for Annie to hand him their Renaissance angel resting in solitary splendor on the mantel.

"Daddy, I want to put the angel on top."

Annie put a quick stop to that suggestion. "No, Kendall. It would be entirely too dangerous with your father standing on the chair and trying to hold you, too." Annie decided that maybe the imperious tone *was* a VerHollan trait, and tried to soften the disappointment. "You can do it next year when we have a proper ladder." She turned to Jessica. "And Jessica can be the first one to turn the lights on."

Both girls seemed satisfied. It was Daniel who looked at her with a smile and a question. Annie shrugged. It was the first time in twenty-four hours that either one of them had mentioned the future. She'd deliberately focused on the past in an effort not to anticipate a time no one could predict. Now, she felt as though she'd broken a spell and for just a moment she was afraid she might not be able to recapture the magic.

Daniel hopped off the chair and the four of them stepped back to admire their handiwork. Daniel reached toward the mantel and handed Annie the glass of wine that had been sitting there, untouched since the project began.

He leaned toward her and saluted with his glass, "Here's to the present." He turned to the girls. "Happy Christmas, everyone." The same wonderful smile that filled his face and crinkled his eyes told Annie he was as moved by the simple family ritual as she was. She moved a step closer. With his arm around her shoulder and the quick kiss he pressed on her forehead, Annie welcomed the stirrings of hope she'd cherished last night.

It was only when they were apart that the doubts nibbled away at her confidence. And they'd been apart for most of the day. Daniel had been called to a meeting early in the morning. It seemed odd that they would meet on a Sunday, especially when it was so close to Christmas, but Daniel promised to explain later.

She'd taken the girls to church, and they'd walked the neighborhood. It was a pleasant day, but Annie couldn't deny a vague worry. It was an emotion alien to her nature and all the more confusing for it. But she couldn't shake off the certainty that the future had a way of becoming the present. She knew, despite all her fantasies otherwise, that at some point they would have to step out of dreamland and talk about tomorrow. She refused to dwell on it, she tried to keep good their promise to live in the present, but it was easier said than done.

"It's too bad we don't have anything to put under the tree." Jessica's words caught her attention.

Annie leaned over and gave her a hug, whispering, "What about those packages you and Uncle Davis brought back the day you went to the toy store?"

The two dashed off to their room and returned giggling and laden with two large boxes and several smaller ones. Once they were appropriately spread beneath the tree, Jessica, their artist-in-residence, pronounced it perfect.

Daniel suggested a room-service dinner and then mentioned a Christmas special on TV. It wasn't long before the girls were settled down for a quiet hour with hamburgers and Rudolph.

Daniel's part of the suite had the largest bedroom. Besides the bed, bath and dressing alcove, there was also a small living area with a love seat and table and chairs. At the moment the table was set with linen, silver, candles and roses. A serving cart with several covered dishes was next to it.

She grabbed his hand and walked into his arms. "Oh, Daniel, it's lovely. I was wondering why you didn't order anything for us."

"The truth is, this is as close as we get to some time alone together." He took her hands and brought them up to his chest. Sliding his hands to her shoulders he pulled her close, burying his face in her hair, then lifting her chin for his kiss.

Annie smiled as his lips touched hers. A shudder of pleasure rippled through her, erasing her smile, focusing her thoughts on the desire that grew as his lips teased hers. She could feel the heavy beat of his heart, the soft caress of his hands, the urgent appeal of his lips, until her awareness was only of Daniel and the moment.

She lost herself in the feel of him, her hands memorized the strong muscles of his shoulders, the crisp touch of his hair, the rough feel of his cheek against hers.

His passion drew her until she wanted nothing more than to be a part of him in the most intimate sharing possible. This meeting of lips and exchange of kisses was an inadequate substitute, a superficial expression.

This kiss ended with the throbbing, aching realization that it wasn't enough. But as a sense of their surroundings returned, Annie understood that it was all the moment would allow. The twilight, the evening sounds, the Christmas music, filtered through, mixing with the passion and mellowing the demand. Annie stood in his arms, trying to capture the intimacy they'd created and hold it in a special place in her heart; someplace where she could call on it and relive the unity, even when they were no longer together.

She ended the embrace as she'd started it, stepping out of his arms and holding his hand. Daniel followed. As she sat down, he pulled his chair a little closer as though he felt the same need to cherish the moment.

The candlelight captured them in its gentle halo. The soft fragrance of the centerpiece—roses, baby's breath and evergreen—added to the fairy-tale ambience at once romantic and seasonal. The setting was far more private than the previous night's restaurant dinner. But the sounds of the television and the girls' giggles were enough to remind Annie that they weren't completely alone.

Last night had been a fantasy. Tonight was reality; no less intoxicating, but far less intimate. As the silence stretched between them, Annie searched for something to talk about. It wasn't that the quiet was unnerving, it just gave her imagination too much freedom to run wild.

She needed a distraction. She glanced at Daniel, who wasn't eating at all but studying her. His slight smile, his intense eyes—all conveyed the invitation of a lover. He needed a distraction, too. Passion held them in a magical dimension where nothing existed but each other and their mutual longing.

They'd come to eat dinner, but for a moment the meal was the farthest thing from her mind. Realization crept up on her like a slowly expanding balloon. Soon the thought filled her consciousness. It was too soon, she thought, but undeniable in its reality. Annie VerHollan loved Daniel Marshall.

Chapter Nine

I love you, Daniel. Annie thought the words, trying them out for size and feel. They fit just right, they felt perfect, but still she was afraid to voice them out loud.

She glanced at Daniel, trying to gauge his possible reaction. He was watching her, waiting. Was it what he wanted to hear? How could he possibly be interested in her when the VerHollans had caused him nothing but pain? Maybe he would consider a brief affair, but surely he didn't want anything as sentimental as a declaration of love.

Annie forced her feelings aside. She did her best to dispel the aura that held them and desperately tried to think of something to talk about, something that would give her a little more of him to treasure, yet nothing too personal.

"Is it hard to get used to the big city when you've spent so much time in villages?"

Daniel nodded slightly, smiling. Was it in understanding or agreement? In any case he accepted her choice, for a moment as both friend and lover. "You've probably spent more time in small towns than I have."

He looked away and the lover faded away completely. His smile was friendly—not impersonal, but not an invitation to anything more than conversation. "I had meetings in the capital pretty often. Of course it's not even one tenth the size of New York, but it's definitely a city with traffic, pollution. It even has its share of violent crime."

Is that how he saw New York, she wondered. It seemed like an enchanted wonderland to her, especially yesterday when it was snowing. "So what do you miss the most?"

Daniel shivered. "The warm weather."

Annie had to agree with him on that. "And what do you miss the least?"

He looked at the onion soup in front of him. "I can't say I miss the food at all."

"Do you have to cook for yourself? What do you eat?"

"I eat whatever the cook fixes." He shook his head, as if recalling some half-forgotten memory. "I learned early on to eat what's served and not ask questions."

"Pretty exotic stuff, hmm?" Annie visualized him sitting around a campfire, meat roasting on a spit—a primitive but comfortable setting.

"Sometimes, but not always." Daniel warmed to the topic. "I remember once he served up something that I almost refused to eat. I couldn't imagine what it was. It turned out to be his version of meat loaf. I can tell you it was all meat and no loaf. Is there some secret to getting meat loaf to hold its shape? If there is, my cook never mastered it."

"Meat loaf? Here I am thinking you subsisted on some native delicacies. I never thought of meat loaf as having African roots." It was amazing how little she knew about his life-style. His letters had been full of news for the children, and very little that gave real insight into his life.

"Well, I'm not sure meat loaf is as universal as wine or bread, but it's made it to my corner of the world. The thing is, who knows what kind of meat it was. Actually, the cook tries hard to please everyone. And we have pretty diverse tastes."

"Is everyone on your crew American?" She wanted to know if there were any families or maybe some single women. She wanted to know if he would remember her when he left; but then that would be talking about the future.

"There are a few Americans, but mostly the group is European. We all get along surprisingly well. We're so isolated, anything less than cooperation would be intolerable. Besides, we all have the same goal, and similar motivation."

"To get the project done?" *And hurry home.*

Daniel nodded. "And a commitment to the people the project's for."

Annie heard the sincerity in his voice and wondered if she would ever understand a man who felt more of a commitment to some nameless African tribe than he did to his own children. "Where do you suppose that sense of commitment came from?"

He didn't seem to mind the questions, even though his soup was getting cold and their hour was trickling away. Maybe he felt the way she did, that it was better to talk about most anything than let his thoughts run riot. Besides, it was this sort of sharing that deepened the trust between them, so that the undeniable passion was more than a physical longing, but as much a spiritual demand.

"Well, when it comes to commitment, I can only speak for myself, but I've always felt that I owed something for the way I was educated. In high school I was on a full scholarship given to the children of missionaries. And my parents always emphasized the importance of making a contribution. They always said we had so much, we had an obligation to give something in return. The truth is, this project's been my chance to return something to society."

Annie understood that. "That's how I felt about the Head Start Program. I'd grown up with so much. And I wanted to give something back." But her parents had convinced her that there were ways of helping that didn't mean you had to sacrifice family.

She spooned the last bit of soup and wondered about the kind of expectations Daniel's parents had had. "Did you ever think about becoming a minister?"

"Sure, I prayed a lot about it in high school, but I knew early on that I didn't have a calling. I guess I was just too practical. I remember, even as a kid, wondering what good religion would do the natives. I mean we lived with them. And I could see they didn't even have enough to eat or medicine to treat their diseases. I felt positively sacrilegious then, but I think that's part of the reason I was willing to go back to Africa. I wanted to give the natives something that would be of material help."

"In your own way you're a missionary. You just represent modern science."

"Well, Annie, let's not declare me a saint yet. The pay is good and the conditions are far from onerous."

It didn't matter what the pay or conditions were. He'd done something she'd only dreamed about. For the first time in years there was a vague doubt about the choices she'd made. "You're really lucky your parents were so supportive."

"I guess I was. Dad realized that missionary work was a special calling and never expected either one of us to follow in his footsteps."

Annie thought about the difference in their upbringings. Her parents definitely expected her to follow in their footsteps. It never occurred to them that she or the children would ever leave Avon. How different her life would have been if her parents had shared the Marshall perspective on family. But the VerHollans believed family was meant to remain an unbreakable unit.

How would her parents react if she made a similar gesture of independence? It didn't bear thinking about. They would never understand. But didn't she deserve the same choices she insisted the twins have? It was so much easier to stick up for the children's rights and deny yourself, especially in a family where martyrdom was touted as a family virtue.

"I wish you could come, Annie. I wish you could see what Africa is like."

Annie almost laughed at the suggestion, but he was serious. He watched with the ghost of a coaxing smile, as though she might really consider a trip to the other side of the world on impulse. It was a testament to his smile that under other circumstances she would have jumped at the invitation. "I'd love to, Daniel, but I don't see how I can. The girls need me and I can hardly take them out of school for a vacation in Africa. I suppose we could come next summer."

Daniel nodded as if he expected exactly that answer. "I'll be home by then."

"Do you really think so?"

He nodded again. "That's what the call was about this morning. They've agreed to hire a new project director. And my boss wanted me to stop in D.C. and go through a preliminary debriefing."

Annie was skeptical. She just couldn't believe his homecoming was imminent. He still had to go back to Africa to actually hire a new director. The trip to D.C. would delay his return to Africa. It would take that much longer to get back on site and prepare for the transition.

Besides, it was difficult to believe that the organization would be willing to accept Daniel's resignation. "And you think that's the only reason they want you to stop in Washington?"

Daniel stood up, moved the soup bowls and served the chicken. All the while he studied Annie, wondering if she was as calm as she looked. Did she even believe him? He felt the ambience of the evening drain away. It had been just as he feared. Any talk of the future was more reality than their newly born relationship could stand.

"No, I'm not that naive. I'm pretty sure they'll sound me out on another project. And I'm just as sure I'm going to turn it down." He'd already made that decision. It would make it that much easier if he went into the meeting with a firm mind. No doubt they were going to offer him some plum to try and tease him back. Another place, another time he might have considered it, but not now. He felt a growing urgency to come home and build a life with his children—and with Annie.

"That may be true, Daniel, but I've spent the last seven years living on the edge of your international life-style. I can't believe you're willing to give it up." Annie looked away, a rejection of his statement implicit in her movement.

Daniel sat back in his chair and moved it just a fraction closer to Annie, as if by doing so he could bridge the gap growing between them. "I've paid my dues, Annie, in more ways than one."

She shook her head, still denying.

He wanted to hold on to the magic, but making her understand was even more important. If they had any future it had to be built on reality. "In your heart of hearts you know I'm coming home. Think about what you've done for the girls. You've spent the last two years preparing them to be my children, to love me."

He'd never really grasped that before. She'd insisted he write, and made the girls do the same. Those letters and pictures were the reason he had daughters who acknowledged him, not the little strangers he'd seen two years ago. It wasn't their eight-year-old maturity that had made him welcome as their father. They loved him now because Annie had made him real to them. "I owe you a lot, Annie—more than you'll ever know."

"I just want you to be a part of their lives."

"Then why won't you believe that I intend to be?" She didn't have to answer. In a flash of insight it occurred to him that she was afraid of losing their love.

Was it possible that Kendall and Jessica had been the focal point of her life for too long? "You know, you've given me something wonderful, but you've given yourself something, too. The kids and I could settle in Saskatchewan, but you'll always be a part of their lives, just like when I go back to Africa. It's only my presence that will be missing, my love won't move an inch. It's something you carry in your heart and that knowledge is liberating."

He spoke the last few words with clear emphasis, wishing the sheer force of his conviction would make her understand.

"Annie, their love for you won't ever disappear."

"I know that."

He sat back in his chair. She might know it intellectually, but he was damn sure she wasn't emotionally convinced it was true. It shouldn't be that hard for her. She was the one who had shown him. How could it be that he needed to tell her this?

He shook his head. The answer wasn't so hard to figure out. All those years of parental indoctrination couldn't help but influence her. And to Wallace and Lillian VerHollan, leaving home meant rejecting their love.

How could he even consider an intimate relationship with another VerHollan? He knew well enough that it was a no-win situation. Their life-style and values were at the opposite extreme from his. Was he on the verge of making the same mistake he'd made before?

He'd been so sure that Annie was different. She'd spent a year in Spain. She'd lived for a while in Augusta. He'd taken those youthful bids for independence as a clear indication that she wasn't going to be limited by her family's traditions. Had it been wishful thinking on his part? He wanted to know desperately. But he wasn't going to find out now. It was clear she was feeling very defensive. Daniel decided to abandon the subject.

"Do you think the girls are up for this evening's expedition?"

Annie was grateful for the change of subject. She'd already lost her appetite. She didn't want to lose her temper, as well. She picked at the last of the chicken on her plate and half listened as Daniel reviewed the plans they'd already discussed two or three times.

Once, not so long ago, Kendall and Jessica were all they had in common. But Daniel's openness had changed all that. She'd accused him of being closed and secretive, and he'd taken her criticism to heart. He'd done his best to be open with her, to answer all her questions. He'd lost his patience once or twice, but he'd never refused.

So, why did she doubt his statement? He was going to return and assume custody of the children. Why couldn't she accept it? Where was the triumph? Hadn't she spent the last two years trying to convince him that that was where he belonged?

Maybe that hadn't been her goal, after all. In all honesty, she'd spent two years trying to convince him that he should be a father to his children. But she had never suspected that he'd want to assume sole custody. She wasn't anxious to get rid of the girls. She just wanted them to know they had a father who loved them and cared for them. Someone who was more than a name on some stupid blank check.

What if he really did come back? What would it be like to lose the girls to his care? What about the twins' grandparents? Her parents would never forgive her for instigating this whole thing. What was the chance they would ever be willing to admit that Daniel was everything a father should be?

How had she gotten herself into this mess? And how would she get herself out of it?

"Then I thought we could stop for a treat on the way back."

"Sounds okay to me," she said, although she obviously hadn't been listening. She glanced at her watch. "Would it be okay with you if the girls talked to Mother and Daddy tonight? If you don't think it's a good idea—"

Daniel cut her off with a smile and gentle shake of his head. "Of course it's all right. Do you want to call now before it gets too late and your mother starts to worry?"

Recalling the previous debacle, Annie agreed. "Probably a great idea."

At least she wouldn't have to talk for long. Her mother would definitely prefer to hear from the girls. Annie collected them as the last of the TV show credits flashed by. The three of them gathered on Annie's bed. Once the connection was established and routine pleasantries exchanged, she turned the phone over to Kendall, making her promise to leave some news for Jessica.

It was like listening to a play-by-play call of some sporting event. Annie sat back against the pillows and cuddled Jessica next to her, while Kendall began a recital of every event from the moment they got on the airplane. Kendall's conversation was littered with details Annie had forgotten, a few she'd just as soon not recall and a hundred charming insights into Kendall's feelings about her father.

Annie gave her a full five minutes before interrupting and letting Jessica talk. To Annie's surprise, Jessica's conversation was no less detailed, but with her own special variation on each story. She added details about the size of Davis's apartment, the way the sky looked when it snowed and the color theme they'd used on the Christmas tree. Did Jessica have an eye for detail because Kendall covered everything else, or was it just her nature to observe things that way?

Jessica had very little to say about her father until the end of the conversation. Then she listened a moment and answered, "I don't miss you if I can talk to you, Grandma. Do you think Daddy will call us when he goes back to his house?"

She listened to her grandmother's parting comment, then handed the phone to Annie.

"Lord help you, Annie. So much for involving that man in their lives. Just think how much it's going to hurt those children when he doesn't call. I knew this plan would backfire. I just hope you have some idea of how to help them cope with the disappointment."

Annie hadn't the faintest idea how to handle the next two hours much less the next two weeks. She wanted to snap at her mother, but the girls were still standing close. She swallowed her harsh words, trading them for the beginnings of a headache.

"We'll talk to you Christmas Day, Mama." She winked at the girls. "I expect Mary Jane will be stopping by your house sometime tomorrow with a little surprise." The twins nodded and giggled. "The girls are blowing you kisses. Bye."

She hung up the phone and reached into the night table drawer for a couple of aspirins.

"This is exactly what I need," Annie announced as the four of them set out toward the bus stop. The girls were skipping ahead and Daniel was the only one who heard her. He turned to look at her, clearly waiting for her to elaborate. She shrugged, "After that dinner, a little exercise is just what the doctor ordered."

It was a valid reason, but not the real one. Annie admitted to herself that what she really wanted was a distraction from her own gloomy thoughts. Hopefully this expedition would do just that. Besides it would give them a chance to recapture the pleasure the four of them had shared yesterday, building their snowman and this afternoon when they'd decorated the tree.

She and Daniel had decided on an evening tour of the department-store windows, hoping the crowds would be smaller. The bus took them down Fifth Avenue and proved an ideal way to view the decorations along the way. There weren't many pedestrians about, very few of them paying any attention to the little bit of Christmas in the windows they hurried by. So Annie was surprised at the number of people gathered around the more famous department-store displays.

The waiting lines were roped off from the rest of the sidewalk and the four of them joined the crowd for the short wait. It was a mild evening and Kendall took care of any incipient boredom by chatting with anyone close by, including a panhandler who asked for her spare change.

There were a few couples, obviously on dates. Annie watched them, wondering if they were as lost in their love as she and Daniel had been last night. The occasional couple was the exception though, most were family groups. Annie watched them too, while she waited, wondering if any of them had a history as old as theirs or a future as uncertain.

Daniel put his arm around her as the group moved forward. "There are certainly a lot more people here than I'd expected, but at least everyone's in a good mood." He looked at her out of the corner of his eye. "Well, almost everyone."

He didn't ask and Annie didn't volunteer the reason for her poor spirits. She did smile at him though and then they turned their attention to the children and the windows in front of them.

They moved through the first display, vignettes of Christmases past based on themes from children's books.

When the girls found a window with a scene from the *The Little Princess* they were ecstatic. Jessica clapped her hands in pleased surprise, "Ooooh, it looks just like I thought it would." She stood transfixed until Annie urged her along. Then the child turned to Annie and explained her fascination with the story, "See, if someone loves you, they'll always find you, just like Daddy found me and Kendall."

Annie turned around to see if Daniel had heard, to share the comment with him, but he and Kendall had moved on to the next scene and were now separated by two or three other small groups.

Was that why the story had meant so much to them? Did they want to make a life with their father? Of course they did. But Annie was sure they didn't understand all the ramifications of that choice.

Neither she nor Daniel had made any concrete plans. Annie wondered if Daniel had ever even discussed it with the girls. She certainly had not. It wasn't surprising, considering the fact that she hadn't been willing to accept his return as the truth. How were they going to tell the girls? Exactly how long was he talking about before he returned for good? One month or six? Even if he gave her a date, she knew from past experience how tentative his plans could be.

Surely finding a new supervisor would take months. And then Daniel would have to train the new employee. Only after all that was done could he give any serious thought to finding a new spot for himself.

Who knew how long that would take or where he would wind up? It could easily be another year before he was ready for full-time parenting. By that time the girls would be prepared and her parents, too, she hoped. At least now she knew she could handle it if the girls were to move away. Daniel's words at dinner had echoed around and around in her head until she finally accepted the truth of them. Kendall and Jessica would always love her. It didn't matter where they lived, she would always be a part of their lives.

She looked ahead to where Kendall and Daniel were waiting for them. He laughed at something Kendall said and took her hand, moving toward the display. He turned from the window, obviously looking for Annie and Jessica. When he caught sight of her, he smiled that wide, cheek-creasing grin that warmed her to her toes.

She didn't see how she fit into the equation at all. There wouldn't be any time to build on this brief holiday romance. In twelve months it would be ancient history.

That hurt more than all her other sorry thoughts combined. A holiday romance. It sounded so sophisticated. What a trite way to sum up the time they'd shared.

She refused the description. What an inadequate label for the past few days. They'd started out as virtual enemies. It hadn't been an easy truce for either one of them. And that truce had given way to a whole new understanding that left them on the verge of still more discovery. The longing she felt wasn't one-sided. It was an invitation, an adventure she welcomed with every part of her. It made her want to laugh, shout, cry. To label it something as banal as a holiday romance was an insult to both their feelings.

Last night had been a taste of paradise. Where had it gone? That wasn't so hard to answer. It had faded in the light of day, in the face of reality. She stared at the final scene, a re-creation of *The Polar Express* and wondered how she could put the magic back into the night.

Fairy godmothers came in odd packages. It was Kendall who granted her wish. As they began to walk to the next department store some ten blocks away, Annie's niece looked back and pulled her father to a halt. When Annie and Jessica caught up with them, she took Annie's hand and put it in her father's. "Let's everybody hold hands and walk together."

Daniel took Annie's hand with a smile. They were walking down a quiet side street, between the avenues. There weren't any fabulous store windows. The shops were closed and dark, the office buildings were locked and guarded. There was only Daniel walking beside her, holding her hand, keeping her close. Layers of doubt, flashes of anger, confusion, faded away. With his touch came a quiet, sure joy. There weren't any crashing cymbals or falling stars, but a certainty that this feeling would outlast any holiday celebration.

Every Christmas memory she'd ever had couldn't begin to compare with the treasure she'd discovered with him. She didn't need fancy trees, elaborate gifts or even a surprise snowfall. All she needed was Daniel's hand in hers.

What was it about holding hands that was so satisfying? Daniel squeezed Annie's hand and smiled. It wasn't nearly as personal as the kiss they'd shared before dinner, not nearly as arousing. That kiss had fired his imagination and his body in a way that his most negative thoughts couldn't control. How amazing that the passion could coexist with the anger and the doubts.

But now, holding hands with Annie, those negatives faded away. There wasn't any anger. The doubts seemed vague and ill-formed.

He held Kendall's hand and felt a totally different sense of protection and love. Maybe that's where the secret lay. Holding hands conveyed a world of emotion that transcended the intimate, physical passion of a kiss. Of course there were different kinds of kisses, but there was only one way to hold hands. In that simple gesture was love, protection, sharing, unity, promise, even dependence—the statement that to get along I need your help, with you this close the world is a better place.

Did the wisdom of holding hands grow from the childhood experience or from the adult promise? Or was it just the most basic expression of trust cradled in love?

It was a good thing Annie knew where she was going, Daniel decided. His thoughts left him following her lead. Kendall and Jessica made sure they didn't dawdle. Within fifteen minutes they had joined the brief line at the last store.

"Gee, Daddy, this one is called Christmas Around The World." Kendall turned to the person behind them, "My Daddy lives in Africa." She turned back to Daniel, "Do you think they'll have your village?"

Africa wasn't one of the countries represented, but Kendall forgot her disappointment, fascinated by the clothes, decorations and detail each window represented. Family groups appeared in each tableau with automated figures opening gifts, attending church and welcoming Father Christmas to elegant English town houses and charming Swiss chalets.

The twins exclaimed over wooden shoes stuffed with oranges and Spanish *señoritas* in lacy mantillas. Annie and Daniel had fun just watching the girls.

As promised, Daniel led them to the hotel restaurant for dessert. It was an elegant spot, more suited to a business dinner than dessert with two children. But Daniel had planned ahead and their dessert was served on his earlier order, giving the children no time to get restless.

Hot chocolate sat cooling while the four of them traded samples of the girls' French pastries and the delicate dessert soufflé that Annie and Daniel shared.

"So what was your favorite scene?" Daniel polled each of them with his question.

"I loved them all," Kendall decided.

Annie wouldn't accept that as an answer. "You spent an awfully long time in front of the *Little House on the Prairie* scene. Wasn't that your favorite?"

A spirited discussion followed. Daniel watched them, sipping the chocolate, enjoying the conversation, wondering exactly how foolish it was to consider making this a permanent arrangement.

Wasn't his failed marriage evidence that attraction wasn't enough to sustain a relationship? He watched as Annie teased the girls about their own Christmas adventure. The attraction was potent and undeniable, but it was only part of the love he felt for her. Her bright, vibrant sharing had given him a stronger sense of himself as part of a whole, not some isolated man struggling to make a difference in a world far from his family.

She'd given him his family at no small cost to herself. She was as unselfish as she was loyal, two virtues that worked as much against him as in his favor. Could she ever give up Avon and a family that was the focal point of her life? Which way would her loyalty push her? Was there really a chance he could be her first choice?

"Some of the clothes were pretty." Jessica turned to her father. "My favorite was the mantilla, like the one Annie has at home."

He turned toward Annie, "And where did you find a mantilla in Avon?"

She laughed. "I didn't. I bought it the year I was in Spain. The only people who've ever used it are Kendall and Jessica when they wanted to play dress-up. It really is pretty."

The comment reminded him of her latent sense of adventure, her year in Spain, that first bid of independence. Maybe she would welcome the chance to be free. Maybe there was a chance he could have it all.

Chapter Ten

"Joy to the world, the Lord is come."

The sounds of the choir, and the thousand voices that accompanied them, echoed through the grand vaults and reaches of St. Thomas. The grand Fifth Avenue church was filled for the vigil service. The concentrated joy of the congregation was contagious. Annie sang with her strong, clear soprano and listened for Daniel's voice.

The last chorus echoed away and almost immediately the organ began the recessional. People stood and moved toward the doors, pausing to call out holiday greetings.

Annie didn't move from her seat. Besides the fact that Jessica was asleep in her lap, the emotion of the music still held her. She didn't want to give up the feeling. Daniel sat next to her, Kendall leaning against him.

Annie turned toward him. "Wasn't that beautiful?"

"It was the most wonderful service I've been to in years." He took a deep breath. It was as though the words were pulled from his heart. "I don't think it's just the church, though. It's sharing it, being here with the three of you."

Annie didn't say anything. She couldn't. The music had left her vulnerable and Daniel's words were the last stroke. Tears filled her eyes. Tears of joy, love, happiness—all mixed with a sense of how fleeting such pure feelings were; how special. She shifted Jessica on her lap, reaching in her pocket for a hankie, a slight shrug her only apology.

Daniel turned practical. "Kendall's like a dead weight and my leg is all pins and needles, but I didn't even notice until the music stopped." He glanced back down the aisle. It gave Annie just the moment she needed to blink away the tears and smile. Daniel nodded toward the crowd slowly filing out of the church. "Let's wait a couple of minutes. It'll be easier to carry these two when the crowd lets up a bit."

Annie was amenable. She wasn't anxious to abandon the aura that enveloped them. Outside the doors of the church it might still be Christmas, but there was enough of the real world out there to dim the glow.

The music continued and she hummed along. "Wouldn't it be incredible to sing a solo here?"

Daniel laughed. "If it was my solo it would be more than incredible. It would be unbelievable. People would cover their ears. They'd flee the church. They'd probably double the collection just to get me to stop. I can't imagine anything *worse* than singing a solo here."

Annie was laughing so hard that Jessica complained in a sleep-slurred voice. The giggles subsided and Daniel continued. "Of course now, your solo would be another story. Are you still doing every wedding and funeral in Avon?"

Annie shrugged. "I do enough to keep me busy. But comparing singing in our church at home to singing here is like comparing potato chips and caviar—they're both snacks, but one definitely has more style than the other."

It was Daniel's turn to laugh. She watched him. As the laugh faded the smile remained. *I love you,* she thought, *especially when you laugh like that.* She wished she could spend her life making him smile.

She looked away quickly, hoping he hadn't read her mind. She wanted their last two days together to be as happy as the previous ones. Her maudlin wishes were definitely not the way to do it. "Don't you think we ought to get these two home?"

Daniel glanced back. "I guess so, but the truth is, I hate to move them. Do you think they'd let us sleep here all night?"

"Daniel, I'm not that unselfish. Besides, they'll go right back to sleep if they do wake up."

He stood up, pressing Kendall's head into his coat. Annie followed him out of the pew and turned around to make sure they hadn't left anything behind.

They walked slowly down the aisle enjoying the last of the organ music. As the final notes sounded, Daniel turned to Annie. "Do you think the girls got anything at all out of the service?"

"A lot more than if we'd waited to go tomorrow. I know from last year that once they wake up on Christmas morning all they think about are presents. At least this way they start out with the right idea about why we celebrate Christmas."

"I guess it isn't long before that's lost in wrapping paper and empty boxes."

Annie nodded. They passed through the inner doors and thanked the celebrant in the vestibule. There were two wooden benches by the doors and Daniel gestured toward them. "Why don't I leave the three of you here? I'll come back for you after I get a cab." He paused at the door and cautioned, "It might take a while. Who knows how many cabbies are out on Christmas Eve."

The air was cooler there. It felt good after the crowded church. Annie sat with Jessica on her lap and Kendall grumpy beside her.

It had been a busy Christmas Eve and now she was as ready for sleep as the girls were. She thought back over the day and knew it would be one of her treasured memories. It had begun quietly enough, it was true, but the anticipation of the holiday and the presents to come led to a steady escalation in the excitement level. Daniel was called to one more afternoon meeting, leaving her alone with two very restless children.

Her mother had called, cheerful and looking forward to the girls' imminent return. Lillian was surprised to hear that Daniel was working on Christmas Eve and Annie carefully explained why it was necessary. Her mother accepted her explanation, but Annie could tell she was unconvinced. She hung up wondering what it would take for her parents and Daniel to make peace with each other. Maybe time, just enough time to let them really get to know each other. And proximity. A little one-on-one would surely help.

The girls had spent hours wrapping and rewrapping the presents they'd bought for their father. There were only a few gifts under the tree. The rest, Annie promised, were on their way from the North Pole. The girls had left a candy bar for Santa and begged the kitchen for a couple of raw carrots for the reindeer. They were as sure as Annie could make them that Santa would know where to leave their presents. By the time Daniel returned from his meeting the girls were full of Christmas and it took both adults to keep their good spirits from exploding into a tantrum. The excitement had taken its toll and the two were now as sound asleep as they could be sitting on a bench in the heart of New York.

Once Daniel claimed a cab it wasn't long before they were back at the hotel and in their suite. The tree was lit when they entered, still with the same few gifts beneath it. But Annie noticed a bottle of champagne nestled in an ice tub and a small tray of some delicacy by the fireplace. She glanced at Daniel, who raised his eyebrows pretending he was surprised, then smiled that sexy, seductive grin that made Annie's fatigue evaporate completely. With the promise of their own private party at hand it didn't take long at all to settle the girls in bed.

When they re-entered the living room Daniel headed straight for the champagne. Annie grabbed his hand and stopped him. "Wait. We have one more chore."

Daniel looked at their coats lying on the floor near the door. Annie shook her head. "No. We have to play Santa."

It took more than one trip to get all the presents from Daniel's closet to the living room. Besides the ones Annie had purchased, there were gifts from her parents, a couple from Davis and some Daniel had obviously added in the past few days.

There were even a couple of big boxes stuffed under Daniel's bed. Annie wiggled under the box springs to pull out the two packages that hadn't fit into the closet. When she stood up Daniel was in front of her and promptly took the boxes and set them on the chair nearby.

He pushed her against the edge of his bed and teased, "I'd much rather have you in my bed than under it." With a gentle pressure he pushed and the two of them flopped onto the mattress.

Annie abandoned all good sense and wrapped her arms around Daniel's neck, pulling him closer. His body pressed into hers and she reveled in the feel of him. Turning her mouth to his, passion exploded between them. The electricity of their kiss held both of them immobile for a moment. Then Annie's body softened and warmed in response to the growing arousal of his. She slid her hands under his sweater and felt his skin heat under her fingers. With a gentle, arousing touch she memorized the feel of him, the play of muscles, the beat of his heart echoing between them. This was sharing, too, an intimate sharing meant just for them. He might be a man of few words, hard won, but all his feelings were easily understood in this moment of silent communication.

Annie relaxed her hold as Daniel trailed kisses down her neck and pressed his mouth in the path of the buttons he was slowly undoing. He cupped her breast with his hand as he kissed her again.

"I love you, Annie. I want you here beside me." Annie wasn't even sure if Daniel had spoken the words. The feel of him next to her, and the growing urgency, were as clear an expression as words whispered in her ear.

"Oh, Daniel, I want you, too." The whisper of passion faded on an unspoken "but." A plea for understanding, a shared regret, a heartfelt promise, all wordless, but understood. It wasn't so much that they doused the flames as banked the fire, each planning to bring it to life later.

Daniel eased himself away and began to button her blouse. He pulled her off the bed and held her in his arms. Annie knew that now wasn't the moment. He would be leaving soon. Who knew how long it would be before she could be with him again? It would be torture to make love then say goodbye.

"What a way to start Christmas." Daniel whispered the words between sweet kisses on her cheek.

Annie nodded. "Somehow, I think the champagne is going to taste awfully flat." Of course, she could think of several different ways to put the sparkle back in the champagne. But by actions if not words they'd both agreed to wait.

Daniel leaned back and looked down at her. "We could save it for tomorrow."

Annie pulled him toward the living room. "No, sir. This is our last chance to enjoy the holiday alone, just the two of us. In just a few hours, Christmas goes wild."

She wasn't ready to abandon the moment. It would happen soon enough. Even if they weren't going to make love now, they could still share the longing, the happiness, the anticipation.

"Those are my sentiments exactly. The thing is, I've got something I'm dying to tell you."

She sat patiently while Daniel opened the champagne with an engineer's precision. A discreet pop and two bubbling glasses later, he joined her on the small love seat. He sat a little away from her and Annie moved closer.

"To the meeting today." He announced the toast and they each sipped their champagne.

It wasn't exactly what she'd expected to drink to, and she waited. Surely there was more.

"The Stateside program directors have agreed to let my deputy take over the project." He watched her, obviously expecting a positive response.

Annie nodded. "That's great." Then she shrugged. "What does it mean?"

He grinned. "It means I don't have to go back to Africa at all." He leaned closer, speaking the words with elated emphasis. "It means I don't have to spend weeks finding someone who can take over the project." He hurried on. "Wyatt already knows as much about it as I do. He even speaks the language better than me. He's been doing most of the local negotiations for months. He can step right in and the program won't be delayed a day."

The words registered, but Annie's emotions were stuck on the announcement that he wouldn't have to go back to Africa.

"You don't have to go back at all?" Annie repeated his words and he nodded. She smiled, imagining a hundred wonderful days and nights before—

"Do you have any idea what you'll do?" She kept the smile plastered on her face. He was so pleased. She didn't want to dampen his enthusiasm. Part of her felt the same excitement. If it had been just the two of them, nothing else would have mattered. But more than the two of them were involved. Someone had to consider the girls, her parents, a whole life they'd built together.

Daniel put his glass down and faced her squarely. "You want to know if I've already made plans?"

Annie nodded, already afraid of the answer.

"Nothing for certain. The point is, Annie, I made that mistake before. This time I want the people I love to have some say." He was watching her and Annie tried to listen with an open mind. "Now, I have to be honest. I've already been contacted by a couple of people. My boss has a friend who's called me twice about a project in Arizona and I'm more than a little interested in a bridge project in Hawaii. You know me and warm weather."

There's warm weather in Georgia. Annie tried to keep her expression neutral, to deny the sense of panic that was rapidly overcoming her happiness. She set her glass of champagne down very carefully.

"What about the girls?" She heard the edge in her voice. Daniel must have, too.

"Oh, Annie." Was it disappointment she heard? Or was he upset because she'd asked the toughest question first?

It might have been the toughest question, but he didn't have any trouble answering it. "They're coming with me."

He was firm, then backed off just a little. "It can't be a surprise to you. It's what I've planned all along. We've talked about it a hundred times this week. I thought you understood." He stopped a moment and then responded to Annie's negative headshake. "I can't believe you don't."

"Do you think that's wise? To uproot them from everything they've known without any preparation, without any transition?"

"What do you think I should do?"

"Come back to Avon with us, spend some time there. Give the girls a chance to get used to the change."

"Annie, the girls are doing just fine. My going back to Avon, without a job, would be like a replay of a bad movie. Not to mention the tension that exists between me and your parents. It wouldn't do anyone any good."

Annie saw the argument coming and was powerless to stop it. All the plans she'd made to ease the transition were pointless. All her hopes for a truce evaporated. Without time there wouldn't be any compromise at all. Daniel had taken away her only bargaining tool.

"What about their grandparents? You weren't here today when they called. They miss the girls. I can't imagine what they'll do if you take them away without warning." *Please understand,* she begged, *please be willing to bend a little.* "The twins are all they have left—"

"Don't say it, Annie." He waved her to silence and the two sat there a moment. Daniel's smile was gone, his teeth clenched. Clearly, it was an effort to control his feelings. "I can't believe you're saying this. You yourself told me that they need their father—"

"Yes, but not at the expense of the rest of their family. Why can't you make peace with my parents? Why can't the three of you find some neutral ground somewhere? Why can't you give me some time to make them understand how wonderful you are, how much you deserve their respect?"

His face softened a little at her words. She sat a few feet away, the span of one soft blue cushion. His expression changed, hardened slightly and that one cushion might as well have been as wide as the ocean.

"I've been that route and I don't think it will ever happen. It's not that I'm unwilling to try, but Lillian and Wallace have seen me as a villain for so long." He shook his head. "I don't think there's much hope of changing that."

"So you're not even going to try? You're just going to take your daughters and leave us with nothing."

He didn't understand. He didn't understand this at all. He looked at Annie and moved a little closer. It didn't work. She edged a little farther back into her corner. He looked at her questioningly, not needing to voice his thoughts.

She shrugged. "I never thought everything would happen this fast, Daniel. I thought it would take months to get everything in place. I mean it always has before. I thought by the time you got back I'd be able to find some kind of compromise—find a way for you to have the girls and to keep my parents happy, too."

It was a pie-in-the-sky wish. But he loved her for wanting it so much. He hated bursting her balloon. "Oh, Annie, honey, I don't think there are enough years in this century to make that happen."

"Then what am I going to do?" She looked defeated and desperate. She looked like a soldier who'd fought against impossible odds and come within an inch of saving the whole platoon.

He knew what he wanted her to do. He knew what would make his life complete. "I guess you're going to have to make a choice, Annie. No matter where you are or where you live you'll always be a part of Kendall and Jessica's lives, but I want more than that. I want you to be a part of my life. The point is, to do that you have to come with us."

She stood for a moment, not moving. He understood the conflict. He tried one more time to convince her.

"You moved out of Avon once. You spent a year in Spain. You've worked hard to give me and the girls a chance to be a family. You've given the girls a way out, why can't you give yourself the same?"

He might know what he wanted, but he also knew which she would choose. Like the soldier, again, she would choose death before a selfish freedom.

She sighed and made her choice. "Daniel, that's the difference between you and me. I know what I want, but I'm not self-centered enough to seize it and forget the feelings of the other people involved."

"But you're willing to sacrifice my feelings, is that it?"

She shook her head. "Don't you think I owe my parents something? They've lost one daughter. They're about to lose their grandchildren. How can I tell them I'm leaving, too?"

"Damn it, Annie. The loss is their choice. It's not like we're traveling to outer space. They can visit, they can call. God knows, your mother perfected that skill these past ten days."

"Yes, and how many times have you talked to her, how many times have you tried to resolve the problem? Face it, Daniel. You don't want to forgive them any more than they want to forgive you."

She folded her hands in front of her and spoke in a low soft voice, laced with bitterness. "That's the truth isn't it? Why Arizona or Hawaii? Did you pick them because they're as far away as you could possibly get from Avon? Surely you could pick a job closer, maybe in Florida or Louisiana."

He didn't answer. He had a sickening feeling of déjà vu, remembered another woman who'd questioned his judgment, questioned his motives.

Annie looked away from him. "So I'm caught in the middle, in a no-win situation. The people who are most important to me can't stand each other."

She stood then, moved away from the sofa toward the door and even further away from compromise. "And now you say I have to make a choice. Well, my parents are going to suffer enough. I can't be a party to separating the children from them. It's what you tried to do before when you went to Africa. And look what a disaster that was."

It was probably the only thing she could have said that made him feel almost as angry as she was. He stood, as well, moved in the direction of his room, putting more than physical distance between them. He faced her without a smile. "If I'm repeating history, so are you." He shook his head and tried to keep the words from pouring out. It didn't work. "Why can't you understand that parents are supposed to encourage other relationships, not stifle them?

"How can you sacrifice what we have on the altar of family responsibility? I thought you were different, Annie.

I thought you and I were on the same track, wanted the same things. I can't believe how wrong I was."

He couldn't believe this was happening. All of his worst fears were materializing. When would she see clearly enough to understand that their love was what their future was all about?

"Oh, Daniel, you make me so mad. I'm telling you and I mean it. I did my best to find a compromise and you've taken every chance we had right out of my hands. I know my family's unreasonable, but now you're being just as bad. That's not the solution I had in mind. It leaves me caught in the middle and miserable. It leaves the children to make choices they shouldn't have to make. I can't believe that makes you happy."

Annie turned and hurried toward her bedroom, past the Christmas tree. That symbol of promise and celebration seemed woefully out of place. Daniel ignored its garish colors and steady lights and watched Annie walk out of his life. With her hand on the doorknob, she turned back to him one last time and whispered, "I guess it isn't going to be much of a Christmas, is it?"

Chapter Eleven

Daniel stood alone in the room. *It's not going to be much of a Christmas.* Annie's words echoed through his head and he turned his back on the tree. It had been the most wonderful holiday season of his life. And now it was a shambles.

The rejection hurt, the loneliness remained; but anger was foremost. The hell of it was, he wasn't sure who he was more angry with—himself or Annie.

He sat down heavily on the love seat, ignoring the holiday decorations, staring into the steady flames of the fire. He wanted to stop the jumble of questions running through his mind, but he couldn't ignore the sense of failure. What had he done wrong? How could he have done it differently? Should he have told her sooner or waited longer?

He thought he'd picked the perfect moment. And it hadn't been easy. He'd waited through an interminable afternoon, waited until after church, waited until the children were asleep, waited a lot longer than he wanted to.

He'd wanted to do it right. There was a lot at stake here. The fact he wasn't going back to Africa had only been part of it, a small part. There was something more important on his mind. He'd wanted Annie to stay in his life. But the argument had begun even before he'd gotten to his proposal.

Exasperation overwhelmed his anger. How could he have been so wrong? She'd seemed pleased enough at first, for a second anyway, before all the implications hit her. Then he'd read panic. She'd come up with all kinds of excuses . . . and never faced the real issue until he'd forced her to.

He felt betrayed.

There was no other way to describe the sense of disappointment. He'd opened himself up to someone for the first time in his life. He'd risked the sharing. All those conversations about family and goals. Did she think it was easy for him? She'd made him confront feelings he'd never examined before, never even been sure he wanted to. He thought they understood each other.

He'd spilled his soul and it hadn't been enough.

Another wave of anger made a seesaw of his emotions. This time in disgust at his own folly. He should have known better. He should have known that this holiday was the stuff fairy tales were made of. Instead, he'd bought into an adult-size version, a happily-ever-after that had more than a little to do with Annie in his life. He built his dreams on the conviction that she understood that growth and change meant taking risks. If he'd learned that in the last ten days, why hadn't she?

Maybe it was easy for her to share feelings and dreams, but that risk had been a giant one for him. Each kiss had convinced him that the fairy tale could be translated into reality. Every time he held her in his arms, heard her laugh, watched her smile, he took one step further from the truth.

Daniel stood up and flipped the switch on the tree lights and then shut off the gas fire. He stood in the dark and listened to the silence. The reality was that only a fool didn't learn from his mistakes. The fact that he stood here right now trying to think of a way to undo the damage made it even worse.

"No, honey, I really don't want to open the rest of my presents, now. This one you gave me is so special, I think I'll just enjoy it for a while." Annie looked up and smiled, or tried to. "Actually, I think maybe we all should get dressed, hmm?"

"Okay, but first we gotta arrange everything in a neat pile so the tree looks pretty again." Jessica took the unaccustomed role of director and urged Kendall into action.

Annie sat back, relieved the girls hadn't noticed her false front. She looked over to where Daniel sat and then looked away just as quickly. He was watching her intently, as though he could read her mind.

In that brief glance she'd seen in his face the same pain she felt. But she also read determination and conviction. Tears welled up in her eyes. If he'd seemed a little more inclined to compromise, she would leave the girls to their chore and spend the time with Daniel, sorting things out. Instead, she followed Jessica's direction and gathered the paper and ribbons, glad that the girls, at least, couldn't see through her.

Her pile of presents didn't need much arranging, all but one were still neatly wrapped and ribboned. She just didn't have enough actress in her to open the presents and maintain the expected good humor. Her heart was overwhelmed with a sense of loss and her head throbbed with a headache brought on by tears and a restless night.

Surely she'd cried every tear she had last night. She'd cried for herself, for Daniel and for what they were losing. She'd stayed awake hours waiting for Daniel to tap on her door and apologize. With every silent minute she felt their future fade further and further away. By the cold light of morning it was nothing more than an empty space, leaving her heart hollow and hurting.

The three of them were almost finished tidying when Jessica looked toward Daniel. "Daddy, when do you want to open your presents?"

He stood up and moved closer to the group. Annie watched him as he spoke to the twins and avoided looking at her. "I think I'll wait until after breakfast. I tell you what. While you three get dressed, I'll order some brunch."

"We want French toast." Kendall announced her order, Jessica nodded and Annie shrugged her shoulders in agreement. Food was the last thing on her mind.

She slipped into her room, thinking about Daniel's stack of unopened presents. What would he think of the miniature portrait of the girls? He really didn't need it now, not if he was really moving out west and taking Kendall and Jessica with him.

She dressed automatically. The shower eased some of the tension in her shoulders. She went through the routine of applying makeup and putting on her clothes, finding some small consolation in the ritual.

What a mess. All along she'd been sure she was in control of the situation. She was the one who'd started it all. She was the one who was certain she could convince Daniel to be an active father. She was the one who was so sure that given time she could make her parents let go.

What had gone wrong? When had she lost control? When had her dreams become a nightmare? Why hadn't she seen it coming?

Because she'd fallen in love.

She'd let her own growing happiness color her judgment, convince her that she and Daniel *did* think alike, that any two people so drawn to each other had to have the same goals. Now she was face-to-face with the fact that she was wrong. They might want the same thing, the girls' happiness, but the biggest mistake she'd made was assuming that she and Daniel defined the children's happiness the same way.

Now she was discovering that you didn't fall out of love nearly as easily as you fell into it. It was the thought of sacrificing the life she'd glimpsed with Daniel that brought tears to the surface again. She'd given away a little piece of herself and she wasn't going to get it back. Right now she wasn't even sure the wound would heal.

Annie was giving her hair one last swipe with the brush when there was a light tap on the door. Daniel leaned in at her response and she waited.

"The girls are eating, then we're going to open my presents. But first I'd like to talk to you for a minute, if I could?"

"Sure." She shrugged. Tossing the brush onto the dresser, she sat on the edge of the bed. Daniel sat in the only chair. Annie insisted that the tension wavering between them was anger, resentment. It had nothing to do with what had happened the last time they'd been in a bedroom together. It had nothing to do with the heartache that made all the rest of their arguments seem trivial.

Daniel leaned forward a little and spoke quietly. "I know that this may not be the best moment to bring this up, but we really don't have much time left."

If he could be civil so could she. Annie nodded.

"I want to tell the girls today. Give them a little while to get used to the idea that they'll be living with me from now on. The thing is I want you there, but not if it's going to be too hard on you."

At least he didn't doubt he would have her support. At least he understood her enough to know that she would never do anything to hurt his relationship with his children.

She rubbed her head, trying to erase away the vague headache and think of an appropriate response.

"I'll be there, Daniel. I think it's important for them to know that I support the idea. But for one thing, this won't come as a complete surprise. You were right when you said it's what I've been working for all along."

He looked relieved and Annie wondered if maybe he *had* doubted her cooperation. Why should he? She was beginning to feel as though self-sacrifice was her middle name.

"The other thing is that I don't want to drop this on your folks like a bombshell. I know how difficult it's going to be for your parents and I want to know how you think I should handle it."

She would have given him an answer if she could. But she had no idea how to ease her parents' distress. She did know one thing. They would take it better from her than from Daniel. "Don't you think I should tell them?"

"Only if you think that's the best approach. I'm not trying to get out of it. I just want it to be the right time and place. I decided last night that maybe I don't know the right time and place as well as I thought I did."

Annie discounted that. "I don't know about that, Daniel. I don't think there *is* a right time and place for that kind of news."

He nodded and leaned closer still, his hands clasped in front of him. "I do have to go to Washington for that interview. And then I thought I could come to Avon and spend a couple of days packing the kids' things."

Annie nodded, trying to control the tears building in her eyes. When she spoke, she looked away from him and pretended she was all right. "I think we should make our Christmas phone call to my folks early today, then we can tell the girls your news. I'll break the news to Mother and Daddy when we get back to Avon tomorrow night."

That was about as civil as she could be. Annie stood up and walked to the window. She didn't lift the edge of the sheer drape. She just stared at the fine grain of the nylon and wished Daniel gone.

"There's one more thing, Annie." He was standing close behind her, too close.

"What?" She felt sick with wanting and denial.

He put his hands on her shoulders and turned her gently around. "I'm sorry."

He stopped and she looked up at him. Her eyes were full with tears. She couldn't really see his expression, but she could feel the tension in his hands on her shoulders. "If there was any way I could make this easier I would. All I can say is I'm sorry I hurt you. I'm sorry that you can't see your way to making your life with us."

She shook her head, unable to speak, wanting him to stop.

He held her a little tighter. "I thought we understood each other. But I guess I was wrong."

She nodded, then spoke, determined to end the conversation before the tears started again, "I'm not quite finished dressing. I'll be out in a minute so you can open your presents."

Daniel stood outside the door, his own heart bursting with pain. Why had he done that? Did he think that little apology was going to make things easier?

He clenched his fist and moved away from the door. He'd hoped that she would see that his love for her gave him the courage to take risks, to open himself, even if it was just a little. He'd hoped she would see that his love was stronger than anything else they had to face.

His love.

Maybe that was the catch. Annie had never once said she loved him, never spoken the words. Maybe she couldn't forgive him for all the failures that had come before. Maybe the past was too big an obstacle to overcome. If she hadn't said it before, what were the chances she would tell him now, when the past was this close to the present?

"Are you ready, Daddy?" Jessica clung to his leg and hugged it. Did the little girl sense his distress?

He stooped down to her level and swooped her up in his arms. She giggled with delight. "Daddy, please let's open your presents now."

Kendall jumped up from the table. "I'll go get Annie."

A few moments later they were all settled close to the tree.

Daniel made a great show of carefully unwrapping and saving each ribbon and as much of the paper as he could salvage. He remembered the VerHollan tradition of reusing paper year to year. This year all his paper was shiny and new. He looked at the girls as he folded a large sheet. "Whose present should we use this on next year?"

Kendall considered. "We have to wait and see how big the boxes are."

He nodded and finished opening the package. The small leather case puzzled him at first. Then he opened it up and stared. It was a miniature portrait of Kendall and Jessica. It must have been recent because he recognized the dresses they were wearing.

He looked at the girls who were beaming in anticipation.

"Do you like it, Daddy?" Kendall nodded, prompting his response.

"It's the most beautiful present I've ever seen."

Jessica wiggled closer. "Someday I'm gonna paint like that."

Daniel nodded. "I'll bet you will, sweetheart." He looked at Annie, who was sitting a little apart from them.

"That will look really nice on your desk at work, don't you think?" She smiled at the girls. "Just in case Daddy forgets what you're like between breakfast and dinner."

He smiled his gratitude. He worked his way through the rest of the gifts. There were books on parenting and a Christmas tie. Kendall and Jessica had even bought him a Lego set. They insisted it had been Davis's idea.

Annie gave him the best gift of all and it wasn't under the tree. As he opened each present, she made some comment about his future with the girls. Kendall and Jessica didn't seem to notice, but he knew she was laying the groundwork for their later conversation. It was a gesture he cherished. He wanted to tell her so, but was afraid of hurting her more. Maybe later he could tell her, when tears weren't so close to the surface.

Her gesture made a good beginning. Once they talked to Lillian and Wallace they could take the next step. He picked up the parenting book, wondering if the author covered his particular topic or if he was going to have to wing it.

The rest of the morning and early afternoon passed in a predictable round of activities. After his presents were opened, the girls returned to their toys. He enjoyed sharing the day with his children. More than once he found himself staring at the two golden heads, trying to memorize every detail. Then he would remind himself that tomorrow wouldn't be the end of his visit. Today was just the beginning of their life together.

By the time the children and Annie finished their conversation with the senior VerHollans, Daniel realized that he and Annie had returned to the strained behavior of their first few days together. He sat on the love seat, admiring his presents with Jessica, when it occurred to him that they had spent the better part of the afternoon talking to each other through the children, using them as a shield.

That was one way to avoid one-on-one confrontation, but echoes of their heated words still leaked from his memory at odd moments. Snatches of argument would replay and he wondered if there was any truth to the accusations she'd made, or were they just the defensive reaction of someone pushed to the limit. That sense of confusion made him wonder if maybe they needed to make one more attempt to clear the air.

"Daddy, can we help you build your new Lego set?" Jessica stood in front of him holding the box and nodding encouragement.

Wanting to talk to Annie and finding time to do it were two entirely different things. Now would be a great time for Davis to pop in with one of his crazy adventures. That wasn't going to happen today, though. Davis and his baby-sitting skills were in Connecticut trying to ignore the matchmaking attempts of the parents of his current girlfriend.

Kendall came up beside her sister. "Oh, yes, Daddy, let's do it together. Then we can put it with the village you gave us and play with it."

Kendall smiled in anticipation and Jessica stood nearby, her head bent to the side waiting for his answer. At that moment he saw Annie in them and a wave of loss washed through him once again. He took a deep breath and hoped there might still be a chance for them. "I'd love to share my Legos with you. I've never done them before. I guess the two of you are going to have to show me how."

Would he ever be able to deny them anything? He wondered if the parenting books covered that. He wondered if he'd ever have time to read them.

They found a spot on the floor, out of the main traffic pattern, and the twins carefully opened the box. It didn't take Daniel long to figure out that the girls had mastered the intricacies of Lego long ago. He was impressed. He watched them pore over the diagrams and wondered if one of them might eventually show the same interest in engineering he had.

He remembered when he was their age, or maybe a little older, he'd started working with an ancient erector set. He'd loved creating simple machines.

As Daniel watched, they moved through the mechanics of building pretty quickly. The engineer in Daniel was fascinated with the plastic building blocks. He watched Jessica neatly add piece upon piece. At first it didn't look like it was going to come out right, but just like the projects Daniel had worked on, the building eventually took shape and formed a whole without a part out of place.

He examined the information booklet and found that each Lego unit could be added to another unit until an entire system was woven together. He admired the girls' handiwork, tossed the booklet aside and admitted that the whole process was a little like life. All the pieces *did* eventually fall into place.

Less than a month ago, his life had been in a thousand little random pieces, like the plastic-wrapped pack of Legos. It had been hard to believe that all the pieces would ever make a whole again. Now the pieces were falling into place. The only problem was there were a few that didn't fit in neatly. Would it just take a little more time, or was it possible that he'd fit the pieces together wrong? Of course he did have a choice. He could make the pieces fit together any way he wanted. He looked at the fire station the girls had built, its edges finished, its roof complete. Maybe he should look at a few other options.

The afternoon seemed interminable to Annie. It really was the beginning of the end of her special relationship with Kendall and Jessica. But even worse, it was the end of something that had never gotten beyond a beginning.

The word *love* came shaded with a hundred different meanings. She loved the girls, her parents, Mary Jane and even Roy, in different ways. And all were spelled l-o-v-e. It was difficult to believe that what she felt for Daniel could be described the same way. It was so much more empowering in its strength and disabling in its loss—something more special than the mother-daughter relationship she shared with the girls, the friendship she felt for Mary Jane. As much as she cared for them, none of them had the power Daniel had, the power to make her heart soar or ache, to blend longing with the anger, turn hope to despair.

"Annie, Annie, come look at the fire station." Kendall called her from her morose thoughts and Annie walked closer to admire their handiwork.

"You three did a great job."

The girls beamed, satisfied with her praise, but Daniel didn't respond at all.

What was he thinking about? Was he trying to find a way to tell the girls his plans? Was he lost in the same recital of wrongs that had ruined her day?

He looked at her then and smiled. It wasn't just any old smile. It wasn't some random smile he tossed out to satisfy the doorman or the chambermaid. It wasn't even the special paternal smile he saved for his daughters.

No indeed. This was the smile that was for her alone. The smile that said friend and lover and all the variations in between. She hadn't seen that smile for twelve hours, but it seemed closer to a lifetime. Annie smiled back and a tiny little part of the weight on her heart lifted.

He eased himself out of his sitting position on the floor and looked at his daughters. "Aren't you all just about ready for dinner?"

He spoke so normally that Annie wondered for a moment if she'd imagined the look. She glanced at him again, and the lingering curve of his lips, the light in his eyes, told her that his smile was as real as her burdened heart.

Daniel's question prompted a chorus of "I wanna eat."

Annie calmed the girls with a look. "I know you're hungry, but that's no reason to forget your manners. Remember the chef gave up part of his holiday to make this buffet so we want to be on our best behavior and not disappoint the cook."

The girls nodded and began to chatter about their favorite dishes. Clearly the twins were in the full throes of their Christmas high. Daniel urged them toward the door. "Why don't we take our coats with us so we can go for a little walk later. I'll bet there'll be lots of people in the park."

The girls found their coats and bickered over hats and gloves while Annie turned the lights out on the tree and Daniel cleared the empty Lego box and wrappings.

They were almost out the door when the phone rang. The girls were halfway to the elevator and Annie waved Daniel on. "I'm sure it's Mary Jane. Why don't you all go ahead. And don't wait for me. I'm not that hungry anyway."

Annie hurried back into the room, regarding the insistent ring as nothing less than divine intervention. She desperately needed to talk to someone. She was expecting to hear Mary Jane's voice and was completely nonplussed when Davis Marshall greeted her with a chorus of "We Wish You a Merry Christmas."

She was silent for a moment, organizing her thoughts.

"Annie? Are you still there?"

Think happy, she reminded herself. Don't spoil his Christmas. "I'm here, Davis. And a Merry Christmas to you, too."

"How's it going? Did the girls get everything they wanted? What did you think of my present?"

"I haven't opened my presents yet." Honesty came too naturally to Annie. The words were out before she realized how they would sound.

Now it was Davis's turn to be silent. When he spoke, his entire tone had changed. "Annie? What's wrong?"

Annie's deep sigh whispered over the line as she abandoned her halfhearted masquerade.

"Have you and Daniel had a fight?"

"We surely did, Davis."

"How about giving me details, kiddo. I can't help without a few clues."

Annie sat on the edge of the bed, still desperate to talk, but unsure of her audience. "It's Christmas, Davis. I hate to spoil your holiday with my unhappiness."

"The only way you'll spoil my day is if you don't let me help."

"Okay." She sounded as though she was admitting defeat. Annie paused and this time Davis waited patiently. She spoke on a sigh. "First of all, Daniel isn't going back to Africa. For all practical purposes his part in the project is over."

"But that's great news!"

"I thought so, too, at first, but he plans to take the girls with him within the week, and he plans to take a job someplace equally as far."

"Just him and the girls?"

Davis sounded puzzled and Annie knew she would have to tell him everything. "Well, he did say something about wanting me to come, too."

"And you said..." He let the word trail off expectantly.

"Davis, how can I even consider it? My parents need me."

"Annie, you mean Daniel proposed to you and you said no?"

"Davis, that isn't what I said at all. He didn't actually propose. He's taking the girls and moving—"

"I heard what you said, but I don't think that's what all your pain is about. You know the girls should be with him. You told me that yourself." He paused a moment. "Now be honest with yourself, and with me. Are you seriously considering sacrificing your happiness with Daniel because you're worried your parents can't live without you?''

She should have known better. Davis was the personification of a free spirit. How could he understand the pull of family ties? ''It's not that simple—''

''Do you love him?''

She remembered Daniel's look and wouldn't deny the truth. ''Yes.''

''Have you *told* him you love him? Annie, listen to yourself. Baby, you've got to see it long-distance, 'cause I can't come play Cupid. I'm too busy dodging arrows here.''

She smiled at the image. She would love to meet the woman who thought she could pin Davis down. ''No, I haven't told him. I guess I'm afraid to admit it.''

''Maybe you're right, Annie. Maybe you should be afraid. Because once you admit it, you have to make choices—and take chances.''

Annie didn't answer him. She knew that was the crux of the matter.

Davis went on. ''Daniel wants something he's never had before. He wants commitment. He wants to know he comes first.''

Davis wasn't arguing. If anything, his voice was soothing. In spite of that, Annie was beginning to feel very defensive. ''He does come first. It's just that the girls are important to my parents. How can I be a part of something that will take them away forever?''

''Do you really think that will happen?''

''I'm afraid that if he acts on this impulse he'll ruin whatever chance he has to make peace. I don't want that to happen. He's a wonderful person. I want my parents to understand he wants to be a father to the girls. That his reason for coming home isn't some kind of vengeful act. I want the world for him, Davis.''

"Oh, honey, loving someone isn't all giving. It's letting them make choices, as well. Part of the pain is realizing that this reconciliation may never happen. But in the end it's your parents' choice and their loss."

Tears began to build in her eyes as she absorbed the truth of what he said.

"Think about it, Annie. It really is very simple. You just have to be honest with yourself. I can give you advice all day, but until you work it out for yourself it won't be real." Davis promised to call back later, then hung up. Annie sat on the bed caught up in his last words.

Simple? He thought it was simple?

She settled on the bed with her box of tissues close by and thought about his words.

Be honest with yourself.

I love Daniel. He loves me. She thought she would feel better with the admission. But she didn't. Loving Daniel wasn't the problem. It was the choices that went with it that were the challenge.

She thought about her parents and a life she felt bound to, and wondered why she felt that way. Was it what she really wanted for herself? And who said loyalties shouldn't change?

She sat staring off into space, letting her thoughts run randomly. They came to rest with Daniel—his smile, his touch, the wordless communication they shared.

If she loved Daniel did she really have any other choice? The commitment was already there. It was the denial of that commitment that brought such grief. Tears trickled down her cheeks and she smiled.

Davis was right. She just had to be honest with herself, she had to listen to her heart. It was either that, or lie to herself and live in misery.

I love Daniel.

This time the words worked their magic. This time she knew that nothing else was as important as that commitment. She smiled at the thought and the weight on her heart eased. She put the tissues away.

Annie didn't think any further. She acted on a spurt of impulse and rejected all the negatives that had been the foundation of her tears.

She hurried from the room, ran for the elevator and found her three favorite people in the half-filled dining room. They were a charming unit, but they weren't complete without her. She knew exactly where she belonged.

Chapter Twelve

Daniel watched Annie walk across the room and bring light and life into it. The twins were engrossed in their turkey and sweet potatoes and didn't see her at first. Annie leaned close to him and whispered, "Merry Christmas."

His Christmas began at that moment. With those words and that smile he knew she was his best and brightest present. He grinned and every light in the room glowed brighter, every ornament on the nearby tree glittered with special brilliance.

The girls claimed her then. They escorted her through the buffet line and filled her plate with all their favorites. Daniel watched them with a special pride and wondered how he'd ever thought anything was worth life without her. He rehearsed speech after speech and prayed, that this time, he would find the right moment.

By the time they'd finished the main course, savoring the turkey and all the trimmings, the dessert that looked so tempting was more than anyone wanted. The maître d' promised to save some for them and the four set out for one last visit to Central Park.

Sucking on candy canes, a gift from the concierge, Kendall and Jessica hurried Annie and Daniel the few blocks crosstown.

"How can they eat those things after that huge dinner?" Daniel was walking next to Annie trying to keep the girls in sight. Once or twice the twins turned and yelled for them to move faster, but Daniel just waved, pretending he misunderstood their direction.

"Surely childhood isn't that much of a memory?" Annie teased. And Daniel loved the sound. "Don't you remember that you always have room for dessert?"

"But they could have had the trifle."

"Ah, but they didn't want the trifle. Tell me, do you know any eight-year-old in America that would prefer trifle over a candy cane?"

Daniel nodded. "Is that in those parenting books you gave me?" He stopped, despite the girls' insistent calls, and turned to face Annie just to see that smile one more time. "And tell me exactly when am I supposed to find the time to read those things?"

Annie shrugged, her smile turning mischievous.

He nodded. "That's what I figured." He turned to walk on, tucking her hand under his arm. "Let's face it, Annie. I can't live without you."

He could have sworn she whispered, "Maybe you won't have to," but the girls swooped down on them and pulled them toward the Park, effectively ending their conversation.

"We wanna skate, Daddy! We wanna skate!"

He didn't want to disappoint them, but he wasn't even sure the rink was open. They ventured through the park and found that the rink was indeed open, and welcoming holiday skaters.

They all rented skates and Daniel and Annie each took a child and helped them lace their skates.

Here was his chance, he thought. He took Annie's skates and led her toward one of the benches that lined the edge of the ice.

Annie followed obligingly. "Do you want to talk to me?"

Daniel nodded. Annie smiled and shook her head. "Me first," she said.

Daniel read a lifetime of love in the look and leaned against a nearby wall and waited.

She didn't sit on the bench but stood behind it as though she was afraid she might need the protection. The gesture was at odds with the small secret smile and made him wary.

"I've been thinking a lot about what you said today about how sorry you were, and I've thought even more about what I didn't say. I have to admit all that thinking wasn't getting me anywhere except maybe close to the *Guiness Book of World Records* for crying jags."

She stopped a moment. "Then Davis called." Annie walked from behind the bench, a couple of steps closer to him. Her smile grew. "Davis does have a way of getting to the heart of the matter, doesn't he?"

Daniel listened with growing elation. With each move, with each word, he could feel the vice that clamped his heart ease.

"The mistake I made was in thinking that there wasn't anything simple about this situation. I thought I'd created a monster that was going to destroy everything I loved. But Davis helped me see that it really is very simple."

She moved even closer, but not quite close enough for Daniel to take her in his arms. "One very simple fact takes precedence over everything else."

She was weighing and measuring words, trying to find a way to smooth the hurts and he loved her all the more for it. Daniel moved to put his arms around her. He wanted to tell her so much, at the very least that the mistakes weren't hers alone.

"The fact is, Daniel, that I love you. I love you more than anything else in the world."

The last of the two-ton weight that had held her down disappeared. The only thing that kept Annie's feet on the ground was the hug that greeted her words. Daniel's love was freedom and the exhilaration of sharing without bounds. Loving him had expanded her horizons, not limited them. It would be the greatest adventure of all.

She wanted to tell him, but couldn't think of words that would express her feelings. Instead she kissed him and together they shared feelings without words, but as clearly expressed as any dictionary definition.

There was passion promised, but the heart of this kiss was commitment, a binding of hearts that Daniel longed for and Annie had never known she needed. Now she couldn't imagine living without it.

She smiled into his eyes. "I feel absolutely invincible."

He smiled back, but there was a touch of reserve, a hint of doubt that sent a shock of fear through her.

He must have seen the uncertainty because her kissed her quickly. "I love you. You're right, it is that simple." He stepped out of her arms and took her hand. "But I have so much to say. So much that needs to be said."

They sat on the edge of the park bench, surrounded by skaters and didn't see one of them. They did notice Kendall and Jessica who skated by once, then twice and waved at them, calling out their names.

Daniel took Annie's hand in his and sat quiet for a moment more. Finally he spoke. "I've been thinking, too. I've been thinking that I would do anything to make you happy again, to wipe the tears from your eyes."

She shrugged and prayed he wouldn't make promises he couldn't keep.

"You were right when you said that I was as unwilling to compromise as your parents. I guess years of negative behavior is kind of like me and my pipe. You know it's a bad habit, but it takes an act of will to change. Well, it worked with my pipe. The point is, Annie, I'm going to try and find some way to come to terms with your parents. You're worth that much to me. I think if we face this together there's at least a chance it will all work out. It may never be perfect, but I swear to you, here and now, it won't be because of me."

Annie moved closer. "It means a lot that you're willing to try. And if they won't accept you, then they'll have to accept the fact that they lose me, too."

It was hard for her to voice the words and she wondered for a moment if she was promising something she couldn't give. As quickly as the thought came it was replaced with the certainty that the only thing she couldn't live without was Daniel's love.

Daniel pulled her close, into his arms, pressing her against his heart. She could feel its steady beat. His voice was a whisper in her ear; "I don't want it to come to that." He sat back and looked into her eyes, still holding her hands. "I think it's time for you to make the break, but that doesn't mean I want you to lose your parents. I wish I could make it easier. If I could give you any present today, that would be it."

"You and your love are the most wonderful present of all."

"Maybe so," he murmured. They sat for a moment lost in wishes and half-formed plans.

"Annie...." His voice was tentative and Annie looked up. "I'd be willing to spend a little more time in Avon, if you think it would help."

She knew what the offer cost him and loved him all the more for it. "Why don't we wait and see what the situation calls for?"

He nodded and stood up from the bench. He pulled her up and into his arms for a kiss. Then he handed her the skates. "In the meantime, we have some skating to do, presents to open and some big news for the kids."

It was the most beautiful ring she'd ever seen. Annie admired the flash of fire from the marquise-cut stone and looked across the aisle where Daniel was supervising the girls. They wanted to fasten their own seat belts and he stood patiently, waiting while they fumbled.

Annie sat back and closed her eyes. It had been a chaotic week, so busy that New Year's Eve would seem tame by comparison. They'd been right to cancel their original return reservation and spend the week with Daniel in Washington. Between sightseeing and a hundred meetings, they'd been working out their future, together.

The week had given her parents seven more days to get used to the idea that Daniel was the most important person in her life now. Her mother's tearful pleading and her father's taciturn acceptance were as hard to take as always, but with Daniel nearby she was able to see their demands in perspective. She'd made the right decision.

Of course it helped that their friends were so happy for them. Mary Jane insisted they could plan weddings together, since Roy had indeed given her his grandmother's diamond and the two of them were even now arguing over wedding dates. Davis had flown to Washington when he heard the news. He'd taken them all out to dinner at the best restaurant in town.

Despite her disappointment at her parents' behavior, it had been a wonderful week. It was as though Christmas, after such a painful beginning, had lasted seven days in celebration.

Daniel slipped into the seat next to her, just as the attendant began the preflight routine. He grabbed her hand and gave her a quick kiss.

"Ready?" He was talking about lots more than her seat belt.

Annie nodded. "How about you? These next couple of months are going to be hardest on you."

He shifted in his seat and faced her. "I don't know about that. But at least we have some built-in escapes. Like a honeymoon and a house-hunting trip." He leaned closer and touched his lips to hers. Her fingers curled into the lapel of his jacket as she welcomed the caress. The feather-light kiss grew until they both were lost in the sharing and the pleasure.

The plane began to taxi away from the lounge area and they sat back, hands entwined. Daniel glanced at Kendall and Jessica who were intent on the airport activity outside their window.

Annie closed her eyes again and longed for a star to wish on. Let every day start with love, she thought. Let every night end with it. The rest of the world might demand the hours in between, but they would make the time to call their own.

"Don't worry, Annie. It's going to work. I know how upset your parents are right now, but Kendall was right when she told them that they 'could get on an airplane' and come to Arizona anytime."

His confidence flagged a little. "I do worry about whether they'll ever be able to forgive the past."

Annie stopped him, pressing her fingers to his mouth. "Shh, when they see how happy you've made me, how committed I am to you, they won't have any doubts." She spoke with such conviction that he relaxed back in the seat and pulled her into the crook of his arm.

The forward process of the plane slowed. With the final announcement of clearance for takeoff, the jet began its race down the runway.

Their adventure was about to begin.

* * * * *

COMING NEXT MONTH

#694 ETHAN—Diana Palmer—A Diamond Jubilee Title!
Don't miss *Ethan*—he's one Long, Tall Texan who'll have your heart roped and tied!

#695 GIVEAWAY GIRL—Val Whisenand
Private investigator Mike Dixon never meant to fall in love with Amy Alexander. How could he possibly tell her the painful truth about her mysterious past?

#696 JAKE'S CHILD—Lindsay Longford
The moment Jake Donnelly arrived with a bedraggled child, Sarah Jane Simpson felt a strange sense of foreboding. Could the little boy be her long-lost son?

#697 DEARLY BELOVED—Jane Bierce
Rebecca Hobbs thought a visit to her sleepy southern hometown would be restful. But handsome minister Frank Andrews had her heart working overtime!

#698 HONEYMOON HIDEAWAY—Linda Varner
Divorce lawyer Sam Knight was convinced that true love was a myth. But Libby Turner, a honeymoon hideaway manager, was set to prove him wrong with one kiss as evidence....

#699 NO HORSING AROUND—Stella Bagwell
Jacqui Prescott was determined to show cynical Spencer Matlock she was a capable jockey. But then she found herself suddenly longing to come in first in the sexy trainer's heart!

AVAILABLE THIS MONTH:

#688 FATHER CHRISTMAS
Mary Blayney

#689 DREAM AGAIN OF LOVE
Phyllis Halldorson

#690 MAKE ROOM FOR NANNY
Carol Grace

#691 MAKESHIFT MARRIAGE
Janet Franklin

#692 TEN DAYS IN PARADISE
Karen Leabo

#693 SWEET ADELINE
Sharon De Vita

INDULGE A LITTLE SWEEPSTAKES

OFFICIAL RULES

SWEEPSTAKES RULES AND REGULATIONS. NO PURCHASE NECESSARY.

1. NO PURCHASE NECESSARY. To enter complete the official entry form and return with the invoice in the envelope provided. Or you may enter by printing your name, complete address and your daytime phone number on a 3 x 5 piece of paper. Include with your entry the hand printed words "Indulge A Little Sweepstakes." Mail your entry to: Indulge A Little Sweepstakes, P.O. Box 1397, Buffalo, NY 14269-1397. No mechanically reproduced entries accepted. Not responsible for late, lost, misdirected mail, or printing errors.

2. Three winners, one per month (Sept. 30, 1989, October 31, 1989 and November 30, 1989), will be selected in random drawings. All entries received prior to the drawing date will be eligible for that month's prize. This sweepstakes is under the supervision of MARDEN-KANE, INC. an independent judging organization whose decisions are final and binding. Winners will be notified by telephone and may be required to execute an affidavit of eligibility and release which must be returned within 14 days, or an alternate winner will be selected.

3. Prizes: 1st Grand Prize (1) a trip for two to Disneyworld in Orlando, Florida. Trip includes round trip air transportation, hotel accommodations for seven days and six nights, plus up to $700 expense money (ARV $3,500). 2nd Grand Prize (1) a seven-night Chandris Caribbean Cruise for two includes transportation from nearest major airport, accommodations, meals plus up to $1,000 in expense money (ARV $4,300). 3rd Grand Prize (1) a ten-day Hawaiian holiday for two includes round trip air transportation for two, hotel accommodations, sightseeing, plus up to $1,200 in spending money (ARV $7,700). All trips subject to availability and must be taken as outlined on the entry form.

4. Sweepstakes open to residents of the U.S. and Canada 18 years or older except employees and the families of Torstar Corp., its affiliates, subsidiaries and Marden-Kane, Inc. and all other agencies and persons connected with conducting this sweepstakes. All Federal, State and local laws and regulations apply. Void wherever prohibited or restricted by law. Taxes, if any are the sole responsibility of the prize winners. Canadian winners will be required to answer a skill testing question. Winners consent to the use of their name, photograph and/or likeness for publicity purposes without additional compensation.

5. For a list of prize winners, send a stamped, self-addressed envelope to Indulge A Little Sweepstakes Winners, P.O. Box 701, Sayreville, NJ 08871.

DL-SWPS

INDULGE A LITTLE SWEEPSTAKES

OFFICIAL RULES

SWEEPSTAKES RULES AND REGULATIONS. NO PURCHASE NECESSARY.

1. NO PURCHASE NECESSARY. To enter complete the official entry form and return with the invoice in the envelope provided. Or you may enter by printing your name, complete address and your daytime phone number on a 3 x 5 piece of paper. Include with your entry the hand printed words "Indulge A Little Sweepstakes." Mail your entry to: Indulge A Little Sweepstakes, P.O. Box 1397, Buffalo, NY 14269-1397. No mechanically reproduced entries accepted. Not responsible for late, lost, misdirected mail, or printing errors.

2. Three winners, one per month (Sept. 30, 1989, October 31, 1989 and November 30, 1989), will be selected in random drawings. All entries received prior to the drawing date will be eligible for that month's prize. This sweepstakes is under the supervision of MARDEN-KANE, INC. an independent judging organization whose decisions are final and binding. Winners will be notified by telephone and may be required to execute an affidavit of eligibility and release which must be returned within 14 days, or an alternate winner will be selected.

3. Prizes: 1st Grand Prize (1) a trip for two to Disneyworld in Orlando, Florida. Trip includes round trip air transportation, hotel accommodations for seven days and six nights, plus up to $700 expense money (ARV $3,500). 2nd Grand Prize (1) a seven-night Chandris Caribbean Cruise for two includes transportation from nearest major airport, accommodations, meals plus up to $1,000 in expense money (ARV $4,300). 3rd Grand Prize (1) a ten-day Hawaiian holiday for two includes round trip air transportation for two, hotel accommodations, sightseeing, plus up to $1,200 in spending money (ARV $7,700). All trips subject to availability and must be taken as outlined on the entry form.

4. Sweepstakes open to residents of the U.S. and Canada 18 years or older except employees and the families of Torstar Corp., its affiliates, subsidiaries and Marden-Kane, Inc. and all other agencies and persons connected with conducting this sweepstakes. All Federal, State and local laws and regulations apply. Void wherever prohibited or restricted by law. Taxes, if any are the sole responsibility of the prize winners. Canadian winners will be required to answer a skill testing question. Winners consent to the use of their name, photograph and/or likeness for publicity purposes without additional compensation

5. For a list of prize winners, send a stamped, self-addressed envelope to Indulge A Little Sweepstakes Winners, P.O. Box 701, Sayreville, NJ 08871.

© 1989 HARLEQUIN ENTERPRISES LTD.

DL-SWPS

INDULGE A LITTLE—WIN A LOT!

Summer of '89 Subscribers-Only Sweepstakes

OFFICIAL ENTRY FORM

This entry must be received by: Nov. 30, 1989
This month's winner will be notified by: Dec. 7, 1989
Trip must be taken between: Jan. 7, 1990–Jan. 7, 1991

YES, I want to win the 3-Island Hawaiian vacation for two! I understand the prize includes round-trip airfare, first-class hotels, and a daily allowance as revealed on the "Wallet" scratch-off card.

Name______________________________

Address______________________________

City____________ State/Prov.________ Zip/Postal Code________

Daytime phone number______________________________
Area code

Return entries with invoice in envelope provided. Each book in this shipment has two entry coupons—and the more coupons you enter, the better your chances of winning!

DINDL-3

INDULGE A LITTLE—WIN A LOT!

Summer of '89 Subscribers-Only Sweepstakes

OFFICIAL ENTRY FORM

This entry must be received by: Nov. 30, 1989
This month's winner will be notified by: Dec. 7, 1989
Trip must be taken between: Jan. 7, 1990–Jan. 7, 1991

YES, I want to win the 3-Island Hawaiian vacation for two! I understand the prize includes round-trip airfare, first-class hotels, and a daily allowance as revealed on the "Wallet" scratch-off card.

Name______________________________

Address______________________________

City____________ State/Prov.________ Zip/Postal Code________

Daytime phone number______________________________
Area code

Return entries with invoice in envelope provided. Each book in this shipment has two entry coupons—and the more coupons you enter, the better your chances of winning!

© 1989 HARLEQUIN ENTERPRISES LTD.

DINDL-3